Spirit Beacon

T. N. TRAINER

AUTHOR T. N. TRAINER

Contents

Chapter 1

I used to wish I was normal. Of course, normal is subjective, but you know what I mean. The desire to be like everyone else is really strong when you're a child. That's when I realized I was different. Seeing your first ghost at six years old is definitely an indicator that something about you is out of the ordinary. I'd been trying to find my way back to ordinary ever since.

My dog, Bandit, stirred in his sleep and growled softly. I wondered what he was dreaming about. He wasn't like other dogs. He wasn't even alive.

One morning shortly after my eighth birthday I woke to find a ghost dog, a black and white border collie with a black patch over his left eye, sleeping on the end of my bed. I had never seen a ghost animal before, but I was utterly delighted. My parents, or rather my mother, wouldn't let my brother and me have a dog, so I didn't care that he wasn't flesh and bone. He was special, and all mine for the past fifteen years, and that was all that mattered.

"Morning, Bandit."

Bandit stirred again.

"Roo."

That was his usual greeting. My dog was a talker. I loved that about him.

Early morning light streamed in through my bedroom windows, splashing shadowy outlines of the divided glass onto the hardwood floor. Bandit cracked an eye at me. The one downside to having a ghost dog was that I could never cuddle or pet him. But, as far as I could tell, he was going to be around indefinitely, and I didn't have to pick up poop, so maybe it was a fair trade off.

When I was little, I didn't know seeing spirits was unusual. They liked to talk to me, and seemed lonely. So was I sometimes. It wasn't until my family gave me strange looks and asked who I was talking to that I realized they couldn't see these people. I didn't understand why, because most of the spirits didn't look different, they just felt a little different. After a while I realized that my being able to see, and feel, spirits was what set me apart from everyone else.

My mom didn't like the idea of me seeing things. At first she thought there was something wrong with me, that maybe I needed therapy. I let her chalk my sightings up to having an imaginary friend. It made her happy to think my odd behavior was just an overactive imagination, and my family didn't look at me like I was strange. Or at least not as much.

Everyone else did though. I would forget sometimes that I was talking to dead people and not living ones, and wouldn't realize until I saw people staring at me. I was some weird little girl who sat there talking to herself. Kids at school started teasing me, calling me 'Crazy Cami.' That name stuck all the way through high school.

"Roo."

"I'm getting up, buddy."

Even spirit border collies had the urge to move things along. Bandit was good at making sure I wasn't late for anything.

I took a quick shower, threw on cutoff denim shorts, a t-shirt, and some flip flops. I ran a brush through my wet hair to get all the tangles out, cleaned the blond strands out of my brush, then grabbed my purse and keys. Bandit ran through the front door of my last century Craftsman beach house. He was sitting patiently on the passenger seat of my light blue 1966 Ford Bronco Wagon before I even got outside. Another perk of having a ghost dog. I didn't have to let him in or out, and there was no chance he was ever going to get run over.

The drive to the little historic downtown of Santa Theresa only took a few minutes. Bandit sat happily on the passenger seat looking out the window, occasionally whining or giving a small bark at something he thought was interesting. I had figured out all his different barks, growls, and other noises pretty quickly. I knew when he saw someone he liked, someone he didn't, something he wanted to chase, something he wanted to investigate, or anything else that was going on with him. For a dog, he communicated like crazy. I knew people who had less to say than he did.

I parked in my usual spot in the cramped little lot that was tucked behind some of the shops that sat on the main downtown street. Most of the buildings in this part of town were Spanish Colonial, white stucco with red shingle roofs, typical of coastal towns in California. They looked clean, neat, and shone in the sun, at least until they needed a new paint job. Salt air had a tendency to wear everything down faster than normal. If you weren't careful, even your car would rust.

I walked around the closest building to the entrance of Beltane Books, the bookstore I had worked at evenings and weekends since I was a freshman in college. They were my only free hours since I had classes at the university weekdays. A huge picture window graced the front of the store, the name of it stenciled on the glass in green with a black trim. Through it I could see displays of books and goods staged to tempt the strolling tourist and local alike. The bookstore was one of the most popular stores in old downtown.

The bell above the door chimed as I entered.

Wizard, my boss's enormous, fluffy, pewter grey Maine coon, peered down at me indifferently from the bookshelf to my left.

"Good morning, Wizard," I said like I did every time I came to work. It seemed somehow discourteous not to.

Wizard looked down at us with a haughty expression and twitched an ear. That was the most greeting anyone ever got out of him. When Bandit followed me in, Wizard twitched his tail in irritation, then looked away and pretended to ignore us completely.

As far as I knew, Wizard was the only other living being that could see Bandit. His eyes tracked the collie all around the store when Bandit decided he had ants in his pants and ran up and down the length of the store to burn off some ghostly border collie energy. Wizard hissed at him from time to time when Bandit thought it would be fun to chase the huge gray furball around. Why a cat that was almost as big as my dog and could probably take him in a fight, if my dog were real, ran was a mystery to me. It wasn't like Bandit could actually catch him. Maybe it was just part of the cat/dog code.

"Cami, is that you?"

Kat's voice floated toward me from the back of the store. She was in the storeroom, probably getting ready to restock the shelves for the weekend. We did a lot of our business on Saturdays and Sundays when tourists were in town. Santa Theresa was a popular stop for people traveling up and down Pacific Coast Highway. The quaint, historic downtown area offered shops, café's, boutiques, and quirky little antique and souvenir stores that catered to most any taste and interest.

"Yes, it's me," I called out.

The scent of pumpkin-apple drifted throughout the room. Kat had lit a new candle for today to give the store even more ambiance than it already had. Antique bookshelves lined the walls of the store, with the exception of the back wall which housed locked cases, and stood in rows in the center of the space. Antique light fixtures hung from the ceiling, casting a warm glow over the entire store. Antique wood tables Kat had found at estate sales were at the front of the store covered with books, or candles, candies, and other sundries we carried. Posters of first edition covers of literary classics hung on the walls over a few of the cases, tempting customers to pick up something they might not have otherwise discovered. Even if I didn't work here I would probably spend a lot of time at Beltane just because it was so warm and inviting.

We were the only independent bookstore in town, and the only bookstore at all in downtown, so that meant a steady stream of business, especially from the locals. Most of our competitors in neighboring cities had gone out of business over the last few years, crushed under the heel of big chain stores. We had managed to survive because of customer loyalty and good service. It also helped that we had the largest inventory, including some very rare titles, of occult books in the Western United States.

My boss Kat, whose name was Katherine Howard (she loved that she had the same name as one of Henry VIII's beheaded wives), was a witch. Her search for occult books had started out as more of a hobby. When she realized there were a lot of people that were as interested in the subject as she was, and that she could make a lot of money selling her finds not just in the store, but online as well to collectors around the globe, she began acquiring them in earnest. Kat had an uncanny knack for finding them at estate sales, other bookstores that had no idea what they were sitting on, and private collections. Occasionally she sent me to buy books for the store when she couldn't get away.

I put my purse behind the worn, mahogany counter and made my way to the storeroom. Kat was unpacking one of the boxes of books that had arrived yesterday from our supplier. Her red hair was pulled back into a ponytail, which hung halfway down her back, and her pale skin was flushed from hefting boxes around. She must have come in early to get a head start.

"Hey," I said as Kat turned around with a stack of books in her arms. "Need some help with those?"

"Yes, actually, we have another fifteen boxes to unpack, but what I really need is some coffee. Would you mind doing a caffeine run?" she begged as she juggled the books. "I can hardly function right now."

"Sure. What do you want?"

"A cinnamon dulce latte. Oh, and a *pain au chocolat*. I'm starving," she replied as I followed her out of the storeroom. She plonked the books on the old, vintage wooden counter, and fished a twenty out of her purse. "Here. Get whatever you want too." She waved a hand at me before I could protest that I could pay for my own. "Please. Half the time I don't know what I would do without you. The least I can do is buy you caffeine and sugar."

"Thanks." I knew it would be no good to argue. She had an in-grained sense of fairness, a moral compass that always pointed true, and always looked out for those she cared about. "I'll be right back."

Beach Brew was only a few doors down from ours, and the smell of freshly ground coffee beans and warm pastries wafted by my nose before I even got to the door. The smell of coffee and freshly baked anything were some of my favorites.

Rachel, a barista about my age with long brown hair pulled back and twisted into a bun, looked up as the door swung shut behind me.

"Hi, Cami, how's it going?"

"Hi, Rachel. Same stuff, different day."

She chuckled as I approached the counter and glanced at the bakery case, which was filled with pastries and breakfast sandwiches. I debated getting an egg, cheese, and sausage biscuit, but something flaky and chocolaty sounded better.

"I hear you," she said. "What can I get you?"

"A cinnamon dulce latte, a blended iced mocha, and two *pain au chocolat*, please."

"Coming right up."

While Rachel busied herself making the drinks, I glanced out the window at Avenida Mar Hermosa, the main road that ran through historic downtown. Traffic was fairly light since it was still early. In an hour every parking space along the street would be full, and tourists would be wandering in and out of the shops, happily buying a seascape painted by a local artist from the gallery across the street, or homemade fudge from the ice cream and candy shop half a block down. Summer was the busiest time of year, but even now, in September, we still had almost as many tourists as we did in June. That was due in large part to the temperate coastal California weather. It was still in the mid-seventies, and probably would be for another month or so.

I was about to check if Rachel was done, when Deedee, a ghost I had first met when I was a kid, suddenly appeared on the street in front of the window. She liked to wander the downtown area, and would find me when she wanted to talk. Deedee had died in the mid-eighties in a car wreck. It was funny how some spirits tended to appear in the clothes they died in, rather than the ones they were buried in. Deedee's dark brown, jaw length, tight curly hair was tied back from a face the shade of pecan shells with a strip of red cloth, ala Madonna. She wore acid washed denim shorts with a rolled hem, a white, sleeveless shirt with a black, mesh tank top layered over it, and white Reebock women's Freestyle high tops with black, lacy socks peeking out.

When she saw me notice her, she smiled and waved. I waved back, making sure to hold my hand close to my chest so Rachel wouldn't see me waving at nothing. At least there was no one else in the store to worry about. There were already a few people who had seen me seemingly talking to myself more than once and thought I was a little unhinged. I didn't need people I interacted with regularly thinking I was a head case.

"Everything's ready," Rachel said from behind me. Both drinks and pastries were sitting on the counter. "That'll be twelve dollars even."

"Thanks. That was fast."

I handed her the twenty, and after I left a tip in the jar and pocketed the rest of the change, I grabbed the coffees and the bag of pastries, and used my butt to open the door.

"See you soon, Rachel."

"Take care, Cami."

Deedee matched my pace as I walked back to the bookstore. She was fairly solid for a spirit, mainly because she hadn't been dead more than a few decades. Most shades got more translucent over time. Really old ones were often little more than a misty outline.

"Hi, Deedee," I said as I took a sip of my iced mocha. "What's up?"

"Hi, Cami," she replied as she bounced along beside me. Everything about Deedee was energetic. She had been a cheerleader in high school, and belonged to like twenty different clubs and activities too. She was the kind of person, now spirit, that had endless enthusiasm, and an almost overly positive, go get 'em attitude. I liked Deedee. Being around her always made me feel a little lighter, and happier. She was more than just a local spirit to me. Over the years she'd become a good friend.

"I talked to Elsbeth this morning," Deedee said as we reached the door to Beltane Books. "She said she saw some different spirits in town this week. Ones not from around here."

Elsbeth was a shade that wandered around Seaview Park. She was extremely shy, even around other ghosts. It took years before she would speak to me. Even now she kept her conversations with me, and the town ghosts, short. The fact that she had shared information with Deedee meant Elsbeth was unsettled by something.

It was kind of unusual for out-of-town spirits to appear in Santa Theresa. Ghosts tended to stay close to where they died. They were tied to that area, usually because of a traumatic death, or an extreme desire to watch over loved ones. Santa Theresa had a population of less than forty thousand, if you didn't count the students at the University, so people weren't dying every day like they did in large cities. And, the fact that most spirits moved on when they died meant that St. T didn't get very many new ghostly residents. Occasionally spirits would wander in from other areas, but most of the ghosts here were local.

I wondered why Elsbeth was unsettled enough to talk to Deedee. Were the spirits malevolent? Had some of them interacted with her? There were definitely ghosts that had an axe to grind. Some didn't like the living, and others didn't like other spirits. They hated the fact that they were dead, and they wanted to take it out on someone.

Then there were some that just didn't want to accept that they were dead. That was the case with Elsbeth. She was endlessly looking for her daughter, who she thought was lost in the park. Elsbeth had no clue that she had died around a hundred and fifty years ago. She didn't even seem to notice all the new buildings and cars that hadn't existed when she was alive. Pointing them out would do no good. She didn't register them at all.

"Really? Did she say anything about the spirits?"

"No," Deedee said cheerfully as I used my elbow to pull open the door to the bookstore. "Just that there are some new ghosts in town. I was surprised she told me at all. She almost never speaks to me. Unlike old Chester. He talks my ear off."

Chester had run a speakeasy in the roaring twenties. He had met an untimely end when two local gangsters decided to have it out in his establishment after getting tipsy on too many Singapore Slings and Sidecars and he got caught in the crossfire. He was definitely one of the chattiest of Santa Theresa's ghostly residents. He was also one who always kept his ear to the ground. Odds were he would know more than Elsbeth.

"How did Elsbeth seem?" I asked. "I mean, other than focused on her search."

"She seemed kind of...agitated, I guess. I asked her what was bothering her, but she wouldn't really say much more. Just said there were 'melancholy spirits about'."

That was odd. Not just that Elsbeth noticed these new ghosts, but that they were 'melancholy'. What was that supposed to mean? And why were unhappy spirits coming to town? What did they want here? It wasn't like Santa Theresa was a hotbed of spiritual activity. That was one of the things I liked about it. It meant I didn't have to deal with being watched or approached by ghosts as often as I did in places like LA.

"Maybe I'll find Chester and talk to him. He'll probably know something."

"Probably," Deedee agreed. "He usually knows what's going on around town."

Bandit came trotting over at the sound of Deedee's voice, his tail wagging. She was one of his favorite local shades.

"Hi, Bandit," she said enthusiastically as she reached down and scratched him behind the ears. I had to admit, I was a little envious of Deedee. She could touch my dog, but I couldn't. "Who's a good boy, huh? Who's a good boy?"

Bandit gave her one of his happy growls and rolled over to get his belly scratched too. At least there was someone who could give him the belly rubs he loved.

"Have you seen Chester around lately?" I asked.

Chester tended to wander back and forth between where his speakeasy used to be, the old house he used to live in just east of downtown, and the cemetery where he was laid to rest. I didn't really want to have to track him down. It would be easier just to go to where he was currently hanging out.

"The last time I saw him was at the cemetery. He was with some of the others that stay around there. That was about two days ago."

I wasn't a big fan of cemeteries, or hospitals. Cemeteries usually had a dozen or so old spirits that drifted around the place, and hospitals were filled with new ones that were completely unaware of the fact they were dead, and were desperate and confused. The old ones wanted a live person to talk to because they missed being alive, and the new ones wanted you to tell them what was going on and why no one else could hear them. I didn't mind talking to spirits, but some of the ones at the cemetery could be relentless. Sometimes they got cranky if they thought you were snubbing them. Cranky ghosts could get vengeful. Being stalked by an angry ghost that wanted to make my life miserable by wailing at two am every night, or whatever other mischief it could think up, I really didn't need.

"Thanks, Deedee. I'll go after work and see if I can find him."

"Okay. Bye, Cami. I'll see you later."

Deedee walked through the door and disappeared a few feet down the street.

Kat poked her head around a bookcase.

"Deedee came by, huh?"

Kat was the only person who knew I could see spirits. No one in my family knew, and I had never told a single friend for the same reason I didn't tell my family. I knew they would look at me like I was crazy, or a freak. Kat was different. She was also one of the most open-minded people I had ever met. When she overheard me talking to one of the local ghosts one day she just asked me straight out if I was a medium. When I finally got over being dumbfounded, I told her I didn't really see myself as a medium or a psychic, but that I could see and talk to spirits. Not only was she not surprised, because as she told me then she had always known I was a 'sensitive', she thought it awesome.

What surprised me as much as her reaction was how much I felt like some kind of burden was lifted off of me. I had been carrying this secret since I was a child, and it felt good to finally be able to share it with someone. Sharing it and being accepted made me feel a little less like a weirdo.

"Yes," I said. "She stopped by to say hi and let me know there are some out-of-town spirits wandering around."

"Really? That's kind of unusual, isn't it?"

"A little. It's probably no big deal. My guess is some of the recently departed from a nearby town that drifted in and have decided to stay awhile."

"Poor souls. Hopefully they cross over soon."

We continued unpacking boxes until the store opened at ten. I flipped the sign hanging on the inside of the door to 'Open', and then unlocked the till on the register. The usual crowds of tourists drifted in, buying an occasional book, or some of the other items, like crystals and incense, we sold. They kept us fairly busy until late afternoon when things finally started to die down.

As we got ready to close up shop, I thought about my conversation with Deedee again, and my promise to look up Chester. Part of me just wanted to go home and curl up with a bowl of pasta and watch some TV, but another part of me was curious about what was going on with these new spirits. And, if Deedee was right and Chester was lurking around the cemetery, it wouldn't take me long to find him and ask a few questions. I could be home and in my jammies before it even got dark. I didn't like cemeteries after dark. That's when the weird, and dangerous, ghosts came out.

Chapter 2

Parker Lane Cemetery was as old as Santa Theresa itself, which meant it was over two hundred years old. It was originally called something else by the Spanish that had first established the town, but was renamed sometime in the middle of the nineteenth century. The old mission, named after Saint Teresa of Avila, which the town was then named after, was long gone, but the sprawling cemetery had grown steadily along with the rest of Santa Theresa. The oldest graves were next to where the old mission had stood, with newer sections laid out in a grid-like pattern on either side.

Chester was buried on the west side of the cemetery, where most people who died in the early twentieth century were. I parked my car as close to his lot as I could, and got out. Bandit popped out the door and trotted along beside me as I cut across the neatly mowed, grassy rows and in between standing headstones, occasionally sniffing in one direction or another. I sometimes wondered if ghosts smelled to him like corporeal people did to living dogs.

I found Chester perched on his gravestone, a rather elegant granite marker chiseled with his name and relevant dates, chatting with some of the shades of his era that rarely left the cemetery. Like Deedee, Chester still wore the clothes he died in. Black, pressed dress slacks with matching vest, white shirt with arm garters, black necktie, and a starched white apron that went from his waist almost to his knees were the only things he would ever appear in.

Nothing else about Chester changed either. His short, dark hair was parted down the middle and shellacked in place with pomade, and a faint, ever present five o'clock shadow that no amount of shaving would completely erase graced his jaw and cheeks. Chocolate brown eyes framed by laugh lines watched me as I walked along the tombstones.

Chester raised a hand and gave me a wave as I approached. I smiled and waved back.

"Cami. It's been a while."

"Hi, Chester. You got a minute?"

I knew he had all the time in the world, but it never hurt to be polite. Ghosts weren't living people, but they were still people. As far as I was concerned, they deserved the same respect as everyone else.

"For you, toots, I got all the time in the world." He glanced at the other shades that were perched on some of the surrounding headstones. "Go chase yourselves, boys. We'll talk later."

The other ghosts drifted off, and I sat on the gravestone opposite Chester's. I knew its owner, Miss Stella March, didn't mind. She'd passed over long ago, and Chester had assured me the first time we'd chatted in the cemetery that sitting on her tombstone wasn't disrespectful. It still felt kind of weird, but if Chester said it was okay, I figured he knew what he was talking about.

Bandit sat down next to Chester's headstone and looked up at him. He liked the bartender almost as much as he liked Deedee.

"So, what do you want to pick my brains about?" Chester asked while he reached down and absentmindedly scratched Bandit behind the ears for a few moments. Bandit's eyelids drooped a little as he enjoyed the attention.

"I thought you might know something about the spirits that recently wandered into town. Deedee said Elsbeth has seen them. Have you seen them too?"

"As a matter of fact, I have. Saw a couple of those specters yesterday. They ain't right."

Two locals saying these new ghosts were strange in some way had me as unsettled as Elsbeth. What could be wrong with them?

"Really? In what way?"

"They don't want to be here, and not in the way most spirits don't. You know, the ones that want to pass on but somehow can't because they have unfinished business or something." Like Chester. He thought he was here because he decided to hang around, but there was always some underlying reason why ghosts lingered. Until they realized it, they didn't move on. "These ones don't want to be *here*, in Santa Theresa." He leaned forward, his forehead creased as he frowned at me.

"How do you know that?"

"One of them, a man, was kind of upset. He asked me where he was. He had no idea. When I told him, he asked why he was here. As if I would know." Chester shook his head. "Ghosts almost always know where they are, or where they should be. I'm telling you, they're not here because they want to be. Something is *making* them be here."

"But how? How can you force a spirit to be here?"

"I don't know. I tried talking to another one of the other newcomers, a lady, but she just said she had somewhere she had to go. When I asked where, and why, she said all she knew was she had to keep going. Then she wandered off. She wasn't all there upstairs, you get my meaning?"

"You mean, she seemed disconnected somehow? Like she didn't understand what was going on?"

"Yeah, disconnected, that's it," he said, leaning back again. "She didn't have both oars in the water, or even know what boat she was in. Even stranger than most fresh spirits."

"That's not that unusual though, Chester. You know that. New spirits are often confused."

"True, but how often are new spirits wandering around a town they didn't die in, and don't want to be in?"

I didn't have an answer to that. New spirits either passed on a short time after their body died, or they remained where they were until they eventually did. Occasionally spirits would drift, but not usually that far. Where were these ghosts coming from, and why?

"Are you sure she was new?" I asked.

"Pretty sure, yeah. She was like a freshly minted penny, you know? All shiny and uncirculated. Fresh ghosts have that feel to them. It takes a long time to get as faded as old Elsbeth over there in the park."

"Did you happen to see where the ghost you spoke to was going?"

"She was heading north of my house, that's all I know. That's where the pull is coming from. I didn't follow her. Didn't figure there was much I could do for her."

"Pull? What do you mean by that?"

"Yeah. There's a sort of energy, or feeling like something is yanking you."

"Wait, you can *feel* what's pulling her?"

Deedee hadn't said anything about that. If Chester could feel it, could the other local ghosts, like Elsbeth, and were they in any danger? Were they going to end up following it too? I didn't like that thought at all. I had known most of them since I was about seven or eight years old. They had watched me grow up, and I considered them friends. I didn't want anything to happen to any of them.

"Sure, a little, but it's not strong enough to make me want to follow it. And, I don't want to know what's behind that pull. Sounds like trouble, you know?"

I was beginning to agree. What Chester told me was troubling. I needed more information. Why were ghosts being drawn to Santa Theresa? There had to be an explanation, but I wouldn't know what it was until I could find out more. The only thing I had to go on right now was that these spirits could possibly be heading to the north part of town. There was a lot north of Chester's old neighborhood, including a couple of strip malls and a number of housing subdivisions. Nothing, however, that I could imagine would draw spirits. Still, it was something.

"Thanks, Chester. You've been really helpful."

"Anytime, doll face. Don't be a stranger." He patted Bandit on the head one more time. "Bye, pooch. Come see old Chester again."

I climbed into my car and drove home, mulling over what Chester told me. What could possibly be drawing spirits from one place to another? What could be creating this 'pull' he was talking about? How many of these spirits were in Santa Theresa? I had no idea how I was going to find answers to these questions. But if I didn't, who would?

Chapter 3

S undays at the bookstore could either be crazy busy, or occasionally so slow you wondered if the earth's population had suddenly disappeared. Just in case it was a slow day, I grabbed some homework. Kat never minded me studying at work if the store was empty. She knew how much I still had ahead of me to get my masters. I graduated with a BA in Psychology, with minors in literature and criminology, from the University of California Santa Theresa last spring, and was now pursuing a master's degree in Forensic Psychology. Work paid the bills, but it didn't leave that much time for homework, so I studied where and when I could.

The weather forecast was the same as it had been all week, and would be next week. Sunny with temperatures in the mid-seventies. I threw on a UCST t-shirt, board shorts, and comfy flip flops and hit the road. I rolled the window down so Bandit could stick his head out a little, instead of through, and maybe smell the beach breeze. I didn't think he could actually feel the wind in his fur, but it seemed to make him happy anyway.

Kat and Wizard were already at the store when I got there. Pete, an undergrad at the U studying astrophysics, arrived a few minutes after me. We usually had at least three people working on weekends. Pete and I were evening and weekend regulars because of our school schedules. Like me, Pete had a couple of textbooks and a laptop tucked under his arm in case the opportunity to study presented itself. Even though he was still an undergrad, he had a pretty hefty course load.

"Hi, Pete. How's it going? You ace your test last Friday?"

"Hey, Cami," he said as he shoved his stuff onto one of the shelves under the counter. He ran a hand through his unruly brown curls and gave me a lopsided smile. "Yeah, barely. I managed to get an A, although I'm not sure how. Didn't study nearly enough. I thought I was going to bomb out for sure."

"Not a chance. You're too smart for that. Not to mention, I've never met a person who can absorb information off a page like you can. Sometimes I think you can just put the textbook to your head and poof! The knowledge just magically transfers itself," I said, smiling back at him.

A faint, pink blush crept over Pete's cheeks. "Nah. I'm just a fast reader, that's all."

"Don't sell yourself short. You're brilliant. NASA is going to be thrilled to have you one day."

"I sure hope so. Otherwise all of this studying is going to be for nothing."

Kat came out from the back, a box of scented candles in her arms.

"Morning guys. There are donuts in the kitchen if anyone wants one."

There was a tiny kitchen wedged into the back of the store between the bathroom and the storeroom. It was large enough to hold an old, narrow refrigerator, a small counter with a sink and a tiny microwave, and a three-foot square wooden table with two chairs. A cabinet hung on the wall above the sink. That was pretty much all that would fit. It was so small you had to go outside just to change your mind.

"Thanks, Kat. Sounds good," I said, anticipating a crumb donut. They were my favorite, and Kat always made sure she included some. "You want anything, Pete?"

"Chocolate dipped, please."

I grabbed the donuts and handed Pete his on a napkin. I perched on one of the stools behind the counter and enjoyed my sugary goodness while Kat filled the candle display. We sold almost as many candles, chocolates, and other things Kat brought in to tempt customers as we did books.

Kat had a knack for finding small companies that made the most amazing products. A lot of them were local, which made them sell even better, especially to residents of Santa Theresa. I'd had no idea there were so many cottage industries in town until I started working at Beltane Books. Kat's philosophy was, 'A rising tide lifts all boats.' She believed a community that helped each other out would mean success for everyone in the long run. So, she put her money where her mouth was and carried as many local products as she could. There was even honey from a local bee farmer on display. Her generosity, and the fact that residents could find so many local products in one spot, was what brought in a lot of the store's customers.

I finished my donut and helped Kat restock the bookmarks and handmade soaps. The morning was pretty slow, so after I was done, I settled back on my stool and studied for the test I had coming up on Tuesday.

The tinkle of the bell announced we had a customer. I glanced up to see a tall, lanky guy in his mid-twenties enter and look around. He didn't look like a regular townie. His 'I'd Rather Be at Comic-Con' shirt and faded Levi's confirmed my suspicion he was probably a student. There weren't a lot of locals that went to Comic-Con.

I went back to studying again since he seemed to know what he was looking for as he headed to a shelf in the middle of the store. I was almost completely absorbed in my notes again when Kat sidled up to the counter next to me.

"I think that guy needs help," she said in that tone she got when she was on some kind of mission. "You should go see if you can point him in the right direction."

I looked up again and wondered who she was talking about. A scan of the store showed me the tall guy was still the only customer in it.

"Him? He seems fine. He's poking around in the history section."

"Yes, but he seems like he isn't finding what he wants. You can help him with that. I'm sure he would appreciate it."

I wasn't as convinced as she was that this guy needed help, but when Kat got that tone in her voice, there was usually some reason behind it. She wanted me to talk to this guy, although I knew she wouldn't tell me why. Kat got all sorts of weird feelings and premonitions, and when they hit, I just went along for the ride. I knew it was no good arguing. Her mind was made up.

"Okay. I'll see if he's looking for something specific."

I slid off the stool and wandered over to the section he was browsing in. He was reading the back of a book on WWI, his forehead creased in what I assumed was concentration. Or, maybe he was disappointed with the book. His light brown hair was a little overdue for a cut because the front was hanging over his forehead and almost into his eyes as he peered down at the book.

"Hi. Can I help you find anything?"

His head bobbed up, his forehead smoothing over.

"Oh, hi. Um, I'm not sure. I don't really know what I'm looking for. Just sort of browsing for a birthday present for my dad."

"Can I assume since you're in the history section that he's a history buff?"

He smiled at me, and it was then I noticed he had the palest green eyes I had ever seen, even lighter than Kat's. Hers were jade green. His were like this crayon I had when I was a kid called 'sea green.' It didn't really look like the sea, but it was one of my favorites in the box. When I looked closer, I could see a ring of golden-brown flecks around the pupil. His eyes were dazzling.

"Yes, he is actually. When he's not working, he spends a lot of time reading, so I thought I would get him a book for his birthday. You can probably tell from how long I've been here that I'm not sure what to choose."

"Does he have a favorite period in history? Is he more into modern history or ancient history?"

"A little of both, I think. He has several books on World War II, and on the Civil War. He also likes to read about General Patton. But since he already has books on those subjects, I thought I would try something different. This one is about World War I and trench warfare," he said, showing me the book, "but it doesn't seem all that interesting."

"Hmm. Well, since your father has an interest in war, and generals, maybe he would like something about some of history's greatest conquerors." I scanned the bookshelf to my left and found what I was looking for. "This one is about Genghis and Kublai Khan, Alexander the Great, Attila the Hun, Julius Ceasar, and others," I said, taking the book off the shelf and showing it to him. "There are some nice illustrations, and photographs of artifacts, so it's not just boring text."

He took the book I offered and leafed through it. I reached to my right and selected a book I had read when I was an undergrad.

"This is a book of letters written between John Adams and Abigail Adams. It's not about war obviously, but their correspondence gives a fascinating insight into the time when our country was being born. And, it showcases the lost art of letter writing. I mean, everybody just texts nowadays. Or sends a quick email. Back then letters were the only way of communicating over distance, and they were kind of an art form. They were eloquent and beautiful. Well, at least these were," I said, feeling like I was beginning to babble. Why was I talking so much?

"These are great," he said, taking the second book and nearly dropping the one on WWI. He juggled all three books awkwardly for a moment before putting the first volume back on the shelf. "I'm sure he'll enjoy both of them. Thanks a lot. You sure know a lot about history." He gave me an angled look as he got a better grip on the books. "I should have gotten your help earlier," he said, smiling at me again.

I smiled back, and for some reason my face was flushed. Why was I acting like some silly school girl? Men, or at least ones I found attractive, tended to make me nervous. I didn't have a lot of experience with dating. I'd been on a few dates in high school, but never had a boyfriend. I dated a little more in college, and even went out with one guy my sophomore year for a few months, but he broke up with me. I had the feeling he thought I was weird. He wasn't the first person that thought that, especially when they caught me talking to thin air.

"Did you want to look for anything else?" I asked, trying to sound normal, and not nervous, even though I was starting to get tongue tied. I wished for the millionth time that I could just be normal, and confident, but I was pretty sure neither was ever going to happen.

"I think these will be fine," he said. As I started to turn to go back to the front, he noticed my shirt. "Do you go to the U?"

"Yes, I'm a grad student there," I said.

"Me too," he said, giving me a crooked smile I thought was almost more endearing than the other one. He squinted down at the books he was holding for a moment, then back up at me as if he was nervous about looking directly at me. "I'm a second-year intern at the hospital there. I did my undergrad work there, and now I'm interning."

"Oh, wow. That's cool."

Cool? Did I really just say cool? I stifled a groan. I was such a huge dork. A cute guy made conversation with me and I turned into a doofus. Might as well have said 'groovy'. I hoped Kat and Pete weren't eavesdropping on the conversation. I was already embarrassed enough.

"What's your field of study?" he asked. At least he didn't think I was such a dork that he wanted to end the conversation and get out of the store. Or maybe he was just polite.

"Psychology."

I would have said more, maybe told him about my thesis, but my tongue suddenly decided it wanted to stick to the roof of my mouth. It was like I was thirteen again, and just as flustered as when my eighth-grade crush, Joey Hanson, asked me to dance at the spring mixer. I had to get this guy out of the store before I made a real idiot out of myself.

After a pregnant and somewhat awkward pause, he said, "I guess I should pay for these."

"Sure."

I led him to the cash register, wanting to kick myself the whole way. At least my mortification would end soon. He would pay and be on his way, and then I would never see him again. I could go back to being my weird self and stick my nose back in my textbook where it belonged.

I rang up his books, put them in a bag, and handed them to him. I looked into those beautiful sea green eyes again. I couldn't help myself. It was the last chance I was going to get.

"I hope your dad has a nice birthday," I said, hoping that didn't sound totally lame.

"Thanks." He took the bag, and after giving me another knee melting smile, headed for the door. He was halfway there when he stopped, paused for a moment, then turned and came back to the register. Now he seemed almost as nervous as I was as his eyes had a hard time finding my face. "I was wondering, um... if you'd like to go out sometime. Maybe get dinner or something."

My mouth dropped open slightly. He was asking me out? My heart started to hammer. I didn't know what to say. He was cute, but I was a total weirdo, and it would only take one date, maybe two to figure that out. I should just say no. Let us both off easy. I wouldn't worry the whole time that I was being awkward or saying something dumb, and he wouldn't have to sit there across the table from me wondering what he had gotten himself into. I mean, that was inevitably how it was going to end up. It always did.

When I didn't reply because my brain and my mouth couldn't seem to get synchronized, he let out his breath and stepped back. "Sorry, I don't normally do that. I'll let you—

"Sure," I blurted out before my brain could overrule my mouth. "That sounds nice."

"Oh, great," he said, relief coloring his voice. "My schedule is kind of crazy, so I can't give you a day right now, but something should open up this week."

"That's fine," I said. "Whenever works. I'm flexible."

I bit my tongue before I started babbling like an idiot again.

"Good." He gave me a half smile as we stood there just looking at each other for a second. "I guess we should exchange numbers."

"Oh, right," I said. I reached for the small notepad and pen that Kat kept on the counter and wrote down my number. Then I slid it over to him. He took the page I wrote on, then wrote his number on the next. I could see Pete and Kat out of the corner of my eye trying to observe and be unobtrusive at the same time.

"So, I'll call you this week?" he asked.

"Sounds good."

He was about to leave again when he gave me a sheepish grin. "Maybe we should introduce ourselves. At least we'll know who we're talking to."

"Right. Names are good," I said, blushing a little again. Why didn't I think of that? "I'm Cami."

"Nice to meet you, Cami. I'm Wynn." He looked at me a moment longer, then said, "Okay, well, I'll call you. Bye."

"Bye."

As he left, I turned to see Kat and Pete grinning at me.

"Man, and I thought I was an ubernerd," said Pete. "That was like watching a proton and an electron trying to figure out how they're supposed to be attracted to each other. Or a nerd mating ritual. You'd think neither of you has ever dated before."

"Oh yeah? Well then, the next cute girl that walks in here is all yours. Let's see how you do, ubernerd."

"I know I won't do well, but it's gotta be better than that," he said, his grin still fixed to his face. "Besides, I'm not going to ask her out, so I won't have a reason to get tongue tied."

"Yeah, right. I've seen you get tongue tied for no reason at all," I said, teasing him back. That was one thing Pete and I had in common. We often got flustered around members of the opposite sex. It was almost a competition as to who was the bigger wallflower.

"Why did you want me to talk to him?" I asked Kat, deciding I would try to get an unlikely answer out of her anyway. "Did you have some kind of feeling about him or something?"

"Yes," she said.

"And?" I pressed when she just stood there giving me one of her mysterious smiles.

"And he seems like a nice guy. I hope you go out with him."

"That's it? That's all you're going to say about it?"

"Yes," she said again.

She winked at me and disappeared into the storeroom, most likely to avoid any more questions as much as do anything important. Kat believed that certain things were meant to unfold on their own without any guidance or interference. This seemed to be one of those times. It was frustrating as all heck, but I knew I wasn't going to get anything else out of her.

Sometimes you just had to pick your battles.

Chapter 4

I was back at the store the next evening when my phone rang. I looked up from my textbook hoping it wasn't my mother. I wasn't in the mood to talk to her. Most of our conversations left me feeling like a berated kid, or at the very least like I didn't fit into my family, which I didn't. Talking to my mom only reminded me of that.

I needn't have worried because it wasn't my judgmental mother.

It was Wynn.

My mouth was suddenly as dry as a week old donut. I had half expected he would never call. People always said they were going to, but often never did. And, the part of me that hoped he would call didn't think it would be this soon.

I stared at the phone as if I didn't know what to do with it.

"You going to answer that?" Pete asked, eyeing the phone, then me.

"Yes, Nosy," I said, picking it up and sliding my finger across the answer bar on the screen. "Hello?"

"Cami? Hi, it's Wynn."

"Hi. How are you?"

"Fine, thanks. Listen, my schedule opened up for a little while on Wednesday evening. I have a few hours free. Does that work for you?"

It did actually. It was one of my evenings off.

"Yes, I'm open Wednesday."

"Great. Do you want to meet at Pietro's Pizza? It's close to the hospital, just in case."

"That sounds fine. What time?"

"Around 6:30?"

"Okay. I'll see you then."

"I'm looking forward to it."

"Me too. Bye."

As I hung up, I saw Pete grinning at me like a Cheshire cat.

"Let me guess. That was Mr. Tall, Nerdy, and Cute calling?"

"His name is Wynn, and yes, if you must know."

"He called?" asked Kat, her head popping out from behind a bookshelf at the back of the store.

"Yes."

Why were these two so interested in my love life? There were no secrets in this store.

"Did he ask you out?" she said.

"Yes, dinner, Wednesday night."

"Oooh, someplace romantic?"

"No, just Pietro's Pizza. He doesn't have a lot of time."

"Doesn't matter," she said as she joined us at the counter. "He called and wants to see you. That's exciting."

"Why is that exciting exactly?"

"Because you don't get out enough, especially with cute guys. You spend all your time here or at the U, usually with your nose in a book. You need some romance."

"You sound like my mother."

"Sorry about that," Kat said, giving me a sympathetic look. She knew my mother had the bit in her teeth about me still being single and not dating. "That's not my intention. I just don't want you to miss any opportunities to meet someone special."

"I know," I said, smiling at her.

We might have talked more and had a good girl chat about Wynn and my lack of a love life, but Pete was in earshot. It would have to wait for another time.

I went back to studying, occasionally taking breaks to help customers, until it was time to close up. As I slid off the stool to do a sweep of the store to make sure there weren't any books left lying around next to the comfy chairs we had here and there for customers to sit in, I noticed a woman, somewhere in her early fifties, wearing what looked like coral colored pajamas staring at me through the front window. At first I thought she was a last minute customer hoping to sneak in before we locked the door, but she wasn't.

She was a ghost.

Was she one of the ones Deedee and Chester had talked about? No, she couldn't be. From what those two had said, the ghosts they saw were going to wherever the 'pull' Chester had mentioned was coming from. This woman wasn't trying to get anywhere. She was just staring at me as if she was sizing me up.

Who was she? Why was she looking at me?

She couldn't come into Beltane Books because Kat had warded the store against ghosts so that I had a space where they couldn't follow me. She had warded my house too. The only exception was Deedee, and of course Bandit. Kat had figured out a way to let Deedee through the ward around the bookstore because she knew I liked Deedee and considered her a friend, and she wasn't a ghost who made trouble.

I wanted to go out and talk to the woman who was standing there staring at me, but Pete was still in the store, and I didn't want him to see me on the sidewalk talking to thin air. Then he would really have something to tease me about. Maybe I could draw her away. I didn't care if a tourist thought I was crazy.

I started for the door, but when the ghost realized I was coming out she gave me a stern look and dissipated. Apparently, she didn't want to talk. So why was she staring at me?

I decided I wasn't going to worry about it. It did remind me, however, that I wanted to talk to Elsbeth on my way home. Maybe I would get some information from her about the strange spirits that were in town. I only hoped she was more willing to talk this evening than the mystery lady.

Chapter 5

I parked in Seaview Park's small lot and got out, my eyes peeled for Elsbeth. The park seemed as empty as its lot, as I had expected since it was early evening. Seaview was my favorite of Santa Theresa's green spaces, not only because it had an unobstructed view of the ocean, as its name implied, but because it was the only park in town that had no palm trees. Not that I didn't like palm trees, but they were everywhere. This park had California Pepper Trees, Coast Live Oak, California Ironwood and others, but palm trees had never been planted. Maybe that was because the park predated the palm craze.

I strolled the pathways that wound through the fifteen-acre park, Bandit trotting along beside me, but I didn't see Elsbeth anywhere. Bandit sniffed here and there, but didn't have any more luck than I did. I was about to give up when I spotted her on a bench, looking out over the ocean. Usually she wandered the paths calling for her daughter. Today she seemed pensive, her brows drawn together as she stared out at the waves.

I approached her cautiously, not wanting to startle her. She had a tendency to disappear if you frightened her.

"Hello, Elsbeth."

She blinked and looked up at me, frowning a little.

"Hello."

Unlike Deedee or Chester, which were fairly solid spirits, Elsbeth was old enough to have started fading. I could see the shadow of the bench through her navy blue, Victorian era bustle dress. Her chestnut brown hair was braided and coiled on the back of her head, and her heart-shaped face was framed by a ringlet curl on each side that just reached her jaw.

She was over a hundred and fifty years old, and had been haunting the park since her death. Rumor among the spirits was that Elsbeth had died of grief after her daughter went missing and was never found. Her ghost didn't remember her daughter never returned, only that she was lost. Spirits often wanted to right the wrongs that occurred in life. Elsbeth figured that if she could only find her daughter, all would be well.

I sat down gingerly on the bench next to her.

"Do you have a moment to talk?" I asked.

Elsbeth sometimes got agitated if someone distracted her from her ongoing mission, but since she was sitting and staring at the ocean, I hoped I had a chance at conversation. It was moments like these when she was the most in tune to the fact that she was a spirit, and not the woman who had lost her daughter.

Elsbeth blinked at me again.

"Yes, I can spare a moment or two."

"Thank you. I wanted to ask you about the spirits you saw recently, the ones traveling through town. Can you tell me about them?"

"They are newly formed spirits," she said, her eyes losing focus. "They are unhappy at being drawn away from their resting places."

"What do you mean, being drawn away from their resting places? These were spirits that were ready to pass on?"

"Yes," she said, her eyes fixed on me again. "One of them told me they were nearly at peace, before they came here. They wanted to move on to the next realm, but were prevented."

"Do you know how?"

"I do not. I have never seen such as these before. What is befalling them is very wrong."

Elsbeth didn't know why they were wandering either. If she didn't know, who would? She was the oldest spirit in town I knew of.

"Chester said he can feel the pull of what's drawing them. Can you?"

Elsbeth shook her head. "I cannot. I am thankful for that, for I do not wish to discover what they are being drawn to."

I wasn't sure I did either, but I didn't like the idea of spirits being drawn to some place they didn't want to go. Something was robbing them of their free will. It was interesting though, that Elsbeth couldn't feel what Chester could. It seemed the pull only worked on new spirits. Her age made her immune.

Elsbeth stood abruptly, and I knew our conversation was over.

"Have you seen Alice?" she asked, her expression suddenly anxious.

Bandit gave a little whine. He liked Elsbeth, and was sensitive to her feelings.

"No, I'm sorry, I haven't."

Elsbeth had probably asked me that question over a hundred times in the years I had known her.

"I must find her. I cannot imagine where she has gone. My husband must be fretting so. We were due home hours ago."

"If I see her, I'll tell her you're looking for her."

"Thank you."

Elsbeth hurried off, frantically calling her daughter's name. I felt sorry for Elsbeth. She was doomed to repeat this pattern endlessly until she faded away. She would never find her daughter. Either Alice had passed on, or her spirit was trapped somewhere else.

I thought about what Elsbeth had said. The spirits that were coming to town weren't wanderers, or poltergeists, or any other type of ghost you would find roaming our earthly plane. They were the spirits of the deceased that were ready to peacefully move on, but were somehow being captured and drawn to somewhere in Santa Theresa. But where? How? By what?

Suddenly a new question occurred to me.

By who?

Chapter 6

I stared at myself in the mirror, again. I had changed clothes five times already, and still couldn't figure out what to wear to dinner with Wynn. Even though it was a pizza restaurant, I didn't want to show up in my usual shorts, shirt, and flip flops. A dress and heels were too much. Bermuda shorts and a tank top didn't seem right either. I was wearing a skirt with a blue flower pattern on it and a white blouse, and trying to decide if I wanted to ditch this outfit too. My mother had bought the skirt for me, so I was sure she would approve of the outfit, at least marginally. She could always find something to criticize.

I glanced at my watch. I was out of time to decide. I only had a few minutes before I had to leave. Blouse and skirt it was. I slipped on a pair of strappy, low-heeled sandals and decided the ensemble would have to do.

"What do you think, Bandit?"

My dog was lying on the end of my bed, his favorite spot. He was staying home tonight.

He half lifted his head off the bed and gave me a once over.

"Rowwwrrr."

"Thanks for the approval," I said as he resumed his nap. It always amazed me how dogs could just drop into sleep like that.

I brushed my hair again and swept it back into a ponytail, then applied a little mascara and some lip gloss. That was usually the extent of my make-up routine. I rarely bothered with much more. Since Wynn seemed okay with my face plain, I left it that way.

My phone rang as I reached for my keys. My stomach sank. Was it Wynn? Was he going to cancel at the last minute? It wouldn't be the first time a date had canceled on me at the last minute, never to be heard from again.

I braced for the inevitable and picked up my phone.

It was my mother.

I groaned. I didn't want to talk to her, not only because I didn't really have time, but because our conversations were stiff and awkward most of the time. I had my mother's blond hair and blue eyes, but that was where the resemblance ended. We had nothing in common except DNA.

I contemplated dodging her call yet again, but I knew that if I did, things wouldn't go well when I did eventually answer. I sighed. I was just going to have to get it over with.

"Hi, Mom," I said, trying to sound cheerful and failing miserably.

"Cami. For goodness sake. I've been trying to get ahold of you all week."

"I know. I'm sorry. I've been really busy with school and work."

"Yes, that seems to occupy all your time."

I could hear the note of disapproval in my mom's voice. My mother was all for education, but as far as she was concerned college, at least for girls, was meant just as much for finding a quality husband as it was for earning a degree. I had the degree, but not even a boyfriend, much less a husband. My brother met his wife in college, and got married right after law school. My mother couldn't have been prouder. Or happier. My sister-in-law was exactly what she wanted—outgoing, social, and into decorating and shopping. Everything I wasn't.

"What's up, Mom?" I asked, not wanting to get drawn into the usual discussion about my future, and whether a master's degree was really what I needed. My mother thought I should get a job in the film studio my father worked for so I could meet some rich, eligible man and settle down. That had no appeal to me whatsoever.

Both my father and brother were in the entertainment industry. My father was a studio executive, and my brother was an entertainment lawyer. I liked movies and TV well enough, but that wasn't the life I wanted. I was not an LA girl, thriving on fast-paced city life, like my mom and my sister-in-law, even though that was where I grew up.

"Nothing important. I just wanted to call and check up on you. I rarely hear from you. If I didn't call, we would never talk."

I felt a pang of guilt, just as my mother intended. My mother and I were never close. I got along with my dad, but my brother Jackson was the only one in my family I really felt connected to. I think that was because he loved me unconditionally, and we had survived childhood together. I loved him too, although I didn't talk to him much either. He was even busier than I was.

"Sorry, Mom," I said, sounding vaguely contrite as I locked my front door. "Time gets away from me. You know that."

I climbed in my car and turned on the engine.

"I do. Are you going somewhere?" she asked as I shut my car door.

"Yes, I have a date."

"Really? With whom?"

I could hear hopeful eagerness in my mom's voice. I forced down the irritation that was threatening to rise.

"No one you know. Just a guy I met at the bookstore."

"Oh."

The disappointment in my mother's voice was evident. She thought he was just some townie. Not that there was anything wrong with the residents of Santa Theresa, but my mother thought everyone from Saint T was provincial. She was kind of a snob that way. She probably thought Wynn was some loser with no future. Who else would ask me out, right?

For some reason, I felt compelled to set her straight. Why I still felt, on any level, like I needed my mother's approval was beyond me.

"He's a medical intern at the U. He's nice."

"Really?" There was an abrupt shift in my mother's tone. I could see her expression in my head. Her eyes were wide, she had sat up straight, and the conversation had just gotten interesting. "What's his name?"

"His name is Wynn. Listen, Mom, I need to go. I'm on the verge of being late, and I can't talk and drive."

"Of course you do." My mother didn't approve of tardiness or talking while driving unless you had a fancy car like she did where you could talk hands free. "Don't let me keep you. Call me tomorrow and let me know how your date went."

I knew I wouldn't, but I didn't tell her that.

"Sure, Mom. Talk to you soon."

I hung up and backed out of the driveway. I knew my mother was probably running upstairs right now to tell my dad I had a date, and was going to want to know every detail of how it went. Or how I screwed it up.

I drove toward the U since Pietro's was only a couple of blocks west of it. I was sitting at a red light only a mile and a half away when I spotted a spirit walking slowly along the street to my right. It was a middle-aged man wearing brown business suit pants, white collared shirt, a tie, and polished business shoes. He had a half-miserable, half-vacant expression plastered to his face as he trudged down the road. Was he one of these new spirits? Where was he going? I really wanted to find out, but I only had minutes before I was supposed to meet Wynn.

What to do, what to do, what to *do*? This might be my only opportunity to follow one of these spirits and see where it was going. I would finally know where they were being drawn to. But, if I did, I would stand Wynn up, and he might never want to go out with me again. Of course, he might not after tonight anyway.

I sat there, my hands gripping the steering wheel. The spirit was continuing on to my right, and Wynn was off to my left. Right or left? What was I going to do?

The driver behind me blared his horn—the light had turned green while I was musing—and I veered left automatically since I was in the left-hand turn lane. I could still see the ghost faintly in my rear-view mirror. I was dying to know where he was going. At the same time, I really wanted to see Wynn. I liked him. And, there was still a chance I could find out where these spirits were going from Chester or one of the other local shades. I decided against the U-turn I was debating and went to the restaurant.

Pietro's Pizza was crowded, as usual. It was a favorite hangout for students attending the U. The lighting was too dim, half the wooden tables that were covered with red and white checkered plastic table-cloths looked like they were on their last leg, and the pictures of Italian-American celebrities that dotted the walls were faded, but it was somehow cozy and comfortable. Every table was full, the bar was packed, and the noise from the crowd and the streamed music washed over me as I walked in like one of the waves I saw from my window every day. So did the smell of pizza, which got my stomach rumbling.

I scanned the crowd looking for Wynn. He had texted me as I was pulling into the parking lot to tell me he was here and had a table. I finally spotted him in the back of the restaurant in a booth. How he had managed to secure that with this crowd I had no idea.

He stood up from the table as I approached. Not a lot of men did that anymore. His mother had raised him well. I could see two large, red plastic cups with water as well as silverware rolled in paper napkins already on the table.

"Hi," he said, smiling at me. Why were my knees twinging? "You made it."

"Hi, yes. Sorry if I'm a little late. My mom called right when I was leaving."

"Is everything okay?" he asked as we sat down.

"Oh, yes, she just wanted to check up on me. You know moms."

His expression grew solemn for a moment, then he smiled again.

"I do. My mom used to check up on me all the time too."

"Used to?"

"My mom passed away from cancer a few years ago."

"Oh my gosh, Wynn, I am so sorry."

Ugh. Trust me to remind him of something depressing.

"It's okay, but thanks."

"That must have been hard, losing your mom so young."

"It was. I think that's what pushed me toward oncology. I hadn't made up my mind exactly what my focus was going to be until she died. After that it seemed pretty clear."

"Oncology is a good field. You could help a lot of people."

"I hope so. Anyway, I'm glad you're here. Are you hungry?" he asked, steering the conversation in a new direction before it could become morbid. I wished I'd been smart enough to do that.

"Yes, actually. I didn't have time for lunch today."

"Great. What do you like on your pizza?"

"Anything except anchovies. Other than that I'm not fussy." I really wasn't. I ate pretty much anything.

Our server, a guy with close cropped dark hair who looked vaguely familiar, probably because I'd had a class with him at some point, came over a few moments later.

"Hey guys, ready to order?"

"I think so," said Wynn, looking at me, eyebrows raised. I nodded at him, and he continued. "We'll take a medium supreme pizza, a share size Caesar salad, and an order of garlic bread please."

The server scribbled quickly on his notepad.

"Anything to drink besides water?"

"I'm fine," I said.

"Me too," Wynn replied.

"Okay. I'll get your order in and be out with the bread and salad in a few minutes."

"The food here is really good," said Wynn after our server left. "I eat here more than I should."

"It is. I haven't eaten here in a while, but it's my favorite pizza in town."

When neither of us said anything for a couple of moments, I decided to forge ahead with the conversation. I hated awkward silences. Too many of them were a bad omen for any date.

"Wynn is an interesting name. Is it a family name?"

Wynn looked sort of embarrassed and gave me a sheepish grin.

"Okay, I'll tell you, but you have to promise not to laugh." I made an X over my heart with my index finger and his grin widened. "It's short for Darwin. My dad is an evolutionary biologist. Charles Darwin is his hero."

"Really? I love that. I've read Origin of Species. I can see why your dad is a fan. And, I really like the name Darwin."

"You're kidding. Or you're just saying that to be nice."

"I'm serious. Besides, it's still better than my name. I'm named after a flowering shrub."

"Wait, let me guess. Camelia?"

"Bingo. My name is Camelia Rose Mitchell. I'm named after my mom's two favorite flowering plants. Lucky me."

"You are lucky. Both names are beautiful." I could see a faint blush creep over his cheeks. "They suit you."

My tongue made a mad dash for the roof of my mouth again as his blush seemed to jump from his face to mine. I was heading straight for dork mode again. I was saved from making any kind of reply by the reappearance of our server who delivered our bread and salad, along with some plates.

The smell of roasted garlic and melted butter made my mouth water. My empty belly gurgled in anticipation. I snuck a glance at Wynn, but he didn't seem to hear my unruly stomach.

After he dished both of us up salad he said, "You said you're working on a master's degree in psychology. What's your thesis about?"

"Forensic psychology, actually. My proposed thesis is a study on whether childhood experiences and trauma are integral to a person growing up to be a serial killer or not, and whether that, or another issue, triggers their personality disorders."

"Wow," he said, sitting back. "That's pretty amazing. That's going to be some thesis."

"Thanks, although I'm not sure how amazing it is. It's not like I'm ever going to be saving lives like you are."

"You never know," he said, his expression earnest. "Maybe one day, because of your research, serial killers might be able to be identified before they get a chance to act on their impulses. If that's the case, you would be saving a lot of lives."

"Maybe. I mean, that would be great. It's always nice to think your hard work pays off for more than just yourself, you know?"

He regarded me for a moment, his eyes warm.

"Yes, I do."

Our pizza arrived and our conversation was put on hold while we tried to munch on hot cheese and sauce without burning our mouths. As I took a second slice, I saw the same woman in the coral-colored pajamas I'd seen outside the store window a couple of days ago over by the bar area. She was staring at me and Wynn, her brows pulled together, her lips pressed into a thin, angry line. I tried to ignore her, but the intensity of her gaze was unnerving. What did she want?

"How's the pizza?" Wynn asked, almost startling me.

My focus snapped back to him. He glanced over to where the woman was, although I knew he couldn't see her. He must have been wondering if I was staring at someone at the bar. There was a guy there looking vaguely in our direction. I hoped Wynn didn't think I was giving him the eye or something.

"Amazing, as usual," I replied, trying not to seem distracted. I really wished that woman would go away.

"Everything else okay?" He glanced over his shoulder again.

Great. He either thought I was bored with our date, or had seen someone more interesting over at the bar.

"Of course."

We made a little more small talk, but it didn't flow as easily as before. I tried as hard as I could to keep my eyes from drifting over to the ghost and just keep her in my peripheral vision. After his last slice of pizza Wynn excused himself to use the bathroom. The spirit watched him go, then approached the table and took his seat across from me. I just stared at her. I hated it when ghosts approached me in the middle of a public place. I didn't like having conversations with them in front of people, for obvious reasons, but sometimes they just wouldn't take no for an answer.

"Who are you?" she asked, giving me a squinty stare.

"I'm Cami," I half whispered, hoping no one was glancing in my direction. I looked at her more closely than I had when she'd been outside the bookstore. Her wavy brown hair was cut short, but cute and feminine. She had blue eyes, and the shape of her mouth looked oddly familiar.

"How can you see me and hear me?" she asked, her gaze still boring into me.

"I've pretty much always been able to see spirits," I whispered. "Is there any way we could talk some other time, somewhere more private? This isn't exactly convenient for me."

She ignored my request.

"So you're what, a psychic? A medium?"

"Something like that. Please, can we do this another time?"

Several people were beginning to stare. I was having a conversation with myself as far as they were concerned. I knew exactly how I must look to them. Like a complete nut. I gave myself a mental kick. I should have gotten my cell phone out and pretended I was talking on that, but the woman had me so flustered from the prolonged staring that I forgot to.

She pursed her lips.

"Well, that's unfortunate."

"Unfortunate for whom?" I asked, getting frustrated. Just then Wynn reappeared from the bathroom area. "You need to go. Now," I hissed.

She looked over her shoulder for a second, gave me a final glare, and vanished.

Wynn glanced at his empty seat, then gave me a puzzled look as he sat down. The couple that had been staring at me put their heads together and snickered. I hoped he didn't know either of them. I didn't need them to tell him his date was crazy. Of course, he had just seen me whispering at nothing, so they probably didn't need to tell him anything.

I tried to seem as normal as I could and like nothing was amiss, but really, what was the point? You couldn't have the issue I had and expect to have a regular relationship.

"I need to get going," Wynn said, his eyes wandering around the restaurant, then back to the bar area. The guy who seemed like he had been looking in our direction was definitely staring now. He had also witnessed my conversation with nothing. Probably thought I was bananas. Wynn's brow furrowed a little. He started to say something else, but just then the waiter dropped off the check.

"Thanks, guys. Hope to see you again soon," he said as he slid the little plastic tray with the check on it onto the table and left.

Wynn and I reached for it at the same time.

"I've got it," he said, getting out his wallet.

"Let me pay half," I said.

"I won't hear of it," he said. He fished some bills out of his wallet and put them on the tray. "I invited you out. It's on me."

"Thank you for dinner," I replied. I would have said it would be on me next time, but I doubted there was going to be a next time.

"You're welcome. Are you ready?"

"Sure." My heart sank as we got up. I had blown another date with all my weirdness. I fished my keys out of my purse when we got to the parking lot. "Well, thanks again for dinner. It was fun," I said, wanting to get the evening over with as much as he did.

"I'm sorry to cut the date short," he said. "I—

"No worries, really," I said, saving him and myself from having to make any excuses. "I'll let you get going."

"Let me walk you to your car," he said. He was a gentleman, I had to give him that.

"You don't need to, really. I don't want to keep you. Have a good night."

I left him standing there as I hurried back to my car. I didn't want him to see I was hurt. He didn't deserve to feel guilty. He deserved a nice, normal girl.

Unfortunately, that wasn't me.

Chapter 7

A fter my last class of the day, Psychology of Deviance, I walked through the quad wondering if I had time to go grocery shopping before work when I saw another of the strange ghosts. This one was a man in his mid-thirties in slacks, a polo shirt, and golf shoes. He had a vacant look in his eyes, and I could feel his confusion as he tried to orient himself. I wanted to approach him and talk to him, but I couldn't. Not in the middle of a quad crowded with students.

He began to wander in a vaguely northward direction, his steps steady and plodding. I debated following him, but I had no idea how far he was going to go, or how long it would take him to get there. I only had about an hour before I had to be at work. Probably not enough time to follow him to his destination.

As I watched him walk away, a thought occurred to me. If he was orienting himself and just starting on his journey, he had to come from somewhere close. The University Hospital was only a short distance away. Could he have come from there? It was the largest hospital in Santa Theresa, and the most likely place for new spirits to be born.

There was a small chance I might find another new spirit I could actually talk to before they started wandering off to wherever they were going. While there weren't very many deaths in Santa Theresa on a daily basis, the hospital was where most of them occurred. It was my best shot at meeting a new ghost. It was better than hoping to see another one wandering around town.

I decided to check out the hospital instead of buying food. I could pick up a sandwich on the way to work. Grocery shopping would just have to wait until one of my evenings off.

I approached the hospital at the entrance to the ER. The trauma center was the most likely place to find ghosts of the recently deceased. Most car accident victims, and even the rare gunshot victim, ended up at this hospital. People were more likely to die here than anywhere else in town. Not because it was a bad hospital, but just because the most seriously ill and injured people were here.

I stood outside the hospital for a few minutes, reluctant to go further. The architect had made an attempt at making this building more interesting than most hospitals, adding scrollwork in the concrete around the windows, tinted, dark blue glass instead of the normal clear panes, and plant beds along the entire perimeter of the structure so that gardeners could add cheerful color with annuals and flowering shrubs. In the end, for all their efforts, it was still just a really large, very white building. Rows of windows dotted each side, and entrances with long cement overhangs jutted out east, south, and west. Regardless of how inviting it tried to be and innocuous it looked, I didn't want to go in.

I *hated* hospitals. This one wasn't as bad as ones in LA, where I was besieged by spirits almost from the second I walked in the door because of the sheer volume of patients that passed through those places, but it was bad enough. There were still usually enough confused, upset ghosts that wanted me to provide answers to make me want to avoid it. But, if I wanted my own answers, I was going to have to deal with it.

The automatic glass doors to the ER whooshed open. I was greeted by the usual cacophony of people talking, voices over the PA system, the beeping of machines, and the sound of crash carts flying down the hall as doctors and nurses responded to someone coding. I took a deep breath and tried to tune out all the noise. It wasn't easy, but I managed it.

Then I opened myself up to the feeling of spirits. I couldn't just see ghosts, I could usually feel their energy, or I could when they were agitated, nervous, or angry. A spirit like Chester, who was calm and laid back, I would only feel if I was fairly close to him. New, scared spirits almost grated on my nerves.

Strangely enough, I felt nothing. How could that be? There were always at least one or two spirits here. There was one I had nicknamed Lingering Larry because he wandered the halls, checking in on patients, watching nurses, but I didn't see him anywhere.

I walked past the main desk, trying not to draw attention to myself while I looked around. The scrub clad nurses behind the desk had their hands full trying to deal with the relatives of the people that had been ambulanced in for treatment. One woman was on the verge of hysteria as she begged them for information on her husband.

I continued farther into the ER, passing brightly lit, curtained exam areas where the least critical waited to be treated. As I turned a corner, I spotted a sheet covered gurney with a body shaped lump parked under a sign that gave directions to other departments on this floor. I glanced around to make sure I wasn't being watched, and when I saw no one in the hall or at the small, secondary nurse's station that was a few feet away, I peeled back the sheet.

The body was that of the man I had seen in the quad. I was right. He had come from here. There was an enormous lump on his temple from which a nasty looking bruise had begun to spread toward his cheek. Had he been hit in the head by a golf ball? Considering the velocity those things traveled, and the point of impact, it definitely could have been his cause of death. He couldn't have died long ago since his body was still waiting to be taken to the morgue, but his spirit hadn't lingered here. It had succumbed to whatever was beckoning it, and it was on its way.

I snuck around the ER a little more but I still didn't see or sense any spirits. It seemed like the crew with the crash cart did their job. That person had pulled through, at least for now. My next best option was the ICU. Most people there were DNR's, so when their time came, no heroic measures were taken. If I was going to have any hope of finding another spirit of someone recently deceased, it was going to be there. It was probably a slim chance since people didn't die in the ICU on a daily basis, but it was the only chance.

I caught the nearest elevator to the third floor, which was as bright and white as the ER. I always thought hospitals needed a little more color, a little cheer. The only units that had any at all were pediatric units. The rest of the hospital was as bland and boring inside as it was out. Only the scrubs of the nurses and doctors added any life to the place. Even a few prints on the walls here and there would have been nice. This hall only had the usual sign declaring that smoking wasn't allowed, and a faded poster taped to the wall near the elevator advising patients to get a flu shot.

I peered down the hall to my right where the ICU was. Technically, only relatives of patients were supposed to be allowed, but I figured I could sneak in. Hopefully.

I walked quietly down the hall and peeked around the door to the ICU. Two nurses in dark green scrubs were manning the desk. One was typing on her computer, and the other was measuring out a dose of medication into a syringe. Nurse number two was probably going to a patient bed to administer what was in the syringe. The other nurse could be there all day. So much for sneaking in.

There were twenty beds in the ICU, two to a room. I could see the large glass windows of some of the rooms because they faced the desk area and hall. All of the beds were full. Over half had geriatric patients, but two were adults in their thirties or forties, one man who might have been in his fifties, and one bed had the small figure of a child tucked into it. I really hoped the little one pulled through. The spirits of children really got to me. A life ending that soon seemed so unfair, although they were usually the ones who caught on the fastest to the fact they were dead. Children seemed to have an intuition adults had outgrown.

I scanned the ICU, but there were no spirits I could see, or feel. It seemed I was out of luck. Not that I wanted anyone to die, but I needed to talk to a new spirit. I would have to check again another day.

I was about to retreat back down the hall when the sound of soft crying drew my attention to one of the rooms on the right, the one with the woman in her forties. Her family was clustered around her bed. A man approximately the same age, a teenage boy and girl, and an elderly woman, presumably her mother, watched over her, their faces anxious. The heart monitor beeped steadily, but the beeps were coming slower, farther apart. Her heart was giving out.

My stomach twisted. It seemed there was going to be a new spirit in the ICU after all. I wanted to find a ghost, but my heart broke for the family in that room. They were about to lose someone they loved. I debated on whether to leave and hope to find a new ghost somewhere around town, but decided against it. I needed to talk to one of these ghosts about what was going on sooner rather than later, and maybe I could offer some comfort even if I couldn't actually help them yet.

I stepped back and wandered down the hall a little. If the monitor was any indication, she had very little time left, and I didn't want to intrude on her final moments. That was for her family to witness, not me.

I stood there for a few minutes, leaning against the wall, unsure of what to do, when I heard the grating beep of a flatline signal. I waited another few moments, then tiptoed back over to the door and peered into the ICU. Nurse number two was taking the woman's pulse as a final confirmation that the machine wasn't malfunctioning, while her sobbing family watched. I needed no confirmation. The woman's spirit materialized above her body, floating as it got its bearings.

I saw, and felt, the moment she became aware of her altered state. She looked around the room as if she wasn't sure why she was seeing it from this angle. She righted herself, then drifted down to the floor.

The woman sucked in her breath in dismay when she saw her own body. Her specter's shoulder's jerk when she realized she was dead, that her family was mourning her, not praying she would pull through. The inevitable confusion and grief followed. She began to cry, reaching for her husband, her children, her mother, but her hands passed through them. She would never touch them again, not in this world. My heart broke for her as her face crumpled with sobs.

Some spirits were called to the great beyond soon after death, while others lingered a day or two before they were called. It seemed this woman was going to be the former. The specter began to glow, a peaceful expression replacing the grief stricken one, as the transition to the afterlife began. Her shade shimmered, then started to become translucent as it began to pass over. But just as it seemed she was on her way, her expression changed. The glow faded and her spirit became opaque once more. Something had interfered in her transition. I saw her anguished expression, heard her protests. She was now like the other spirits that were wandering through Santa Theresa, trapped here until she reached her destination.

I retreated back down the hall halfway to the elevator, my heart aching for her, and her family. Her family would lay her body to rest, but they had no idea her spirit couldn't. Not now anyway. I felt her getting closer as the siren song only she and the others could hear drew her out of the ICU. She spotted me as soon as she crossed its threshold.

"Hello?" she said when she saw me looking at her. "Can you see me?" she asked, her eyes wide as she approached me.

"I can see you and hear you," I said quietly so the nurses wouldn't overhear.

"I'm Susan. I don't know what's happening to me. I died, but now..."

"I'm Cami. I'm not sure what's happening to you either, although I know it's not just affecting you."

"Can you help me? Is that why you're here?"

I so wished I could say yes to that, but I had no idea what to do for her.

"I'm sorry, I don't know how to help you. I'm still trying to figure out what's happening to new ghosts. All I know is that it started recently."

"I feel so strange," she said, glancing back at the ICU. "I was supposed to go somewhere, somewhere nice I think, but I couldn't get there. Now I feel like I have to go somewhere else. Do you know where I have to go?"

I shook my head.

"I wish I did. There are others like you, spirits going through the same thing you are. They said they feel a pull of some kind. Is that what you feel?"

She thought for a moment, then nodded.

"Yes. It's as if there is something tethered to the center of me and it's tugging at me. I don't want to go, but the tugging is getting stronger." Just as she said that, she took a staggering step forward. "Please, I don't want to go wherever this is pulling me. I want to stay here and go to the other place."

"I know. I'm so sorry." She took another step forward, her brows scrunched together and mouth tight as she tried to resist. I debated what to do for a moment, then decided it wasn't going to be the end of the world if I was a little late for work. Kat would understand if I told her what was going on. "I'm going to follow you so I can see where you're going. Maybe once we get there I'll have a better idea of what's happening, okay?"

"Okay," she said, but her voice was changing, becoming hollow, and her expression became confused and disconnected, just like the others I'd seen. She began to wander away, no longer fighting the pulling sensation. She disappeared through a wall, and I knew I didn't have long to catch up with her.

I hurried over to the elevator banks and frantically pushed the down button, willing the doors to one of them to open. Finally, just as I was going to bolt for the stairs, the middle door opened. I rushed forward, not checking to see if anyone was disembarking.

And ran straight into Wynn.

He was wearing a doctor's coat with *Dr. Caldwell* stitched in black on the left breast, jeans, a blue, patterned, button down shirt, and running shoes. His hair was tousled and still a little too long, especially in front, and he had the bleary-eyed look of someone who had pulled an all-nighter. His eyes widened as he saw me.

"Cami? What are you doing here?"

I froze, my brain trying frantically to come up with some reason why I was in the hospital, much less by the ICU.

"I, um, was observing in the psych ward for a class," I said, utterly relieved I came up with something plausible on the spot. The psych ward was on this floor, albeit on the opposite end of the building. "What are you doing here?" I added, then felt stupid. He worked in the hospital. He had more reason to be here than I did.

"I was coming up to check on a patient I sent up yesterday. She's in the ICU."

"Oh, right. The oncology ward is downstairs now?"

"No," he said, giving me a half smile. "I'm doing an ER rotation right now."

"Right. I forgot interns did rotations."

The elevator door behind him closed. If I didn't take the stairs now, I was going to lose that ghost. She would get too much of a head start on me, and I would never know which part of campus she was drifting through.

"Can I talk to you?" he asked, stepping away from the elevator.

"Um, sure." I really wanted to chase that ghost, but I couldn't think of any reason why I couldn't talk to him. The fact that I had already come up with a good lie under pressure was a miracle. I was pretty sure I wouldn't be able to come up with two. Not to mention, I really didn't like lying to people. I pushed down my frustration. I was never going to find out where those ghosts were going at this rate.

"About last night. I'm sorry if I upset you by leaving early. I got called when I was in the bathroom. The ER was slammed and they really needed me. I should have told you that right away, but I was distracted and thinking about what was going on here. I tried to tell you when we were in the parking lot, but you kind of bolted."

That was why he wanted to leave? Relief washed over me, which was followed by a feeling of chagrin. I had automatically assumed he wanted to end the date because of me and my weird behavior.

"I'm sorry about that. If it's not already obvious, I don't date that much, or that well."

"It's not obvious at all, and don't feel bad. I'm not great at it either," he said, ducking his head a little, his green eyes peeking at me through really long lashes. How did I not notice those lashes before? You could practically stand on them.

"You seemed okay to me," I replied, hoping I didn't get mush mouth again. My nervousness always seemed to affect my ability to talk.

"Oh good. I'm sometimes hopeless at making conversation, especially when I'm nervous."

"You were nervous?"

"Totally. You couldn't tell?"

I shook my head. "No, not at all. I thought I was the only one that was a tongue-tied mess."

"Oh good. I mean, not that you were a tongue-tied mess. Just that I wasn't the only one," he said, his cheeks coloring a little. "So, you think maybe we could try it again?" he asked, a hopeful note in his voice. "Maybe we'll get it right the second time."

"I'd like that."

"Great," he said, a warm smile lighting up his face. "I just traded a shift with someone, so I'm free tomorrow night. Does that work for you? I'm sorry, I know it's kind of last minute again."

"Yes, actually. I work the day shift tomorrow."

"Would you like to do an early dinner, at a real restaurant this time, and a movie after?"

"Sure, that sounds nice," I said, my stomach besieged by a flutter of butterflies. We were going out again, and I was nervous and excited at the same time. I only hoped the second date ended better than the first.

"Okay, I'll pick you up at your place then?"

"I'll text you my address."

"See you tomorrow then."

He smiled and walked backward a few paces before turning and entering the ICU. As I watched his tall, lean frame approach the nurse's station I wished fervently again that our next date went well.

I also realized I had lost another ghost.

Chapter 8

The bookstore was a zoo most of the day. It was a beautiful Saturday, and every tourist within a fifty-mile radius seemed to want to buy a book about Santa Theresa, or a local product, and were coming and going all day buying anything and everything we had out. I had to make frequent trips to the store room to bring out more product. I hoped Kat had already reordered a lot because our stock of local products was running low by early afternoon.

"Did you find everything in the storeroom?" Kat asked. "I know it's a mess back there. I meant to organize it this morning but too much stuff got dropped off yesterday and I couldn't get to it all."

"I managed to find everything. I only have one more display to stock."

"Thanks, Cami. Oh, more local stuff is going to be delivered today too. The bee farmer is coming by, and so is that guy who delivers for most of the others. At this rate we're going to be out of some supplies by the end of the day."

"Good. We're starting to run low on almost everything. I'll restock the back room and out here when it comes in. I hope what gets delivered today is enough to keep customers happy when Darla comes tomorrow."

Darla Woodward was a local author who wrote mysteries and thrillers. Every time she had a new book out, she did signings at Beltane Books. Tomorrow was going to be even busier than today.

"No kidding. I ordered extra just in case. Thanks for taking care of everything, Cami."

I was doing mostly restocking and rearranging the displays because Pete drew the short straw, so to speak. Or lost rock, paper, scissors, actually. I almost always beat him at that, so he was relegated to helping Kat with the customers while I did everything else. Most people would prefer just to answer questions and ring up sales, but I liked to do the busy work instead. Large crowds sometimes made me uncomfortable, and when the store was as busy as it was today, I liked to do something that kept my interactions with them to a minimum. I still helped out, and I answered questions if a customer approached me, but I didn't have to do it almost nonstop like Kat and Pete did. A day like this usually had me completely exhausted at the end if I spent all day talking to people, and since I had a date with Wynn tonight, I didn't want to be wrung out.

I was about to dodge back into the store room for crystals and tarot cards when the bell over the door tinkled.

A pale, dark haired guy wearing a black shirt and black jeans, and sunglasses he forgot to take off, came into the store. Why anyone wanted to be covered head to toe in long dark clothes in this weather was beyond me. It was approaching eighty today, and the humidity was over seventy percent. That guy needed some shorts.

He headed straight for the back of the store, right for the glass cases with locked doors that lined the wall. That was where Kat kept the store's inventory of occult books. I saw him go from case to case, searching for something. He wasn't browsing; he seemed really intent. A weird vibe pinged on my radar about this guy. Some of the customers nearby cast unsettled glances at him and moved to bookcases farther away.

Pete approached him as he was halfway through the cases. At first the man ignored Pete. He looked at every book, his head bobbing up and down as he searched from shelf to shelf. Pete spoke to him, and the man rounded on him like a snake that spotted prey. All the color drained from Pete's face. He must have just gotten the same vibe, only magnified by a hundred. Pete held his ground though. He spoke again, although now his wide eyes gazed at the man with a hint of fear. The man said something else I couldn't hear, and Pete shook his head.

Kat joined them a moment later. If I had a weird vibe about him, I was pretty sure her intuition was in overdrive. She touched Pete on the arm and said something to him. Pete retreated back to the counter area looking pale and shaken. With trembling hands he cashed out the customers that were waiting to pay, one eye still on the Man in Black, and Kat.

Kat spoke to the guy who had scared the crap out of Pete. He took a step back, as if he didn't want to be close to her. He seemed tense during their brief discourse, like he resented his search being interrupted, especially by her. He made a quick comment, the muscles in his jaw bunching up. When she shook her head, his eyebrows clenched together. He balled his hands up so hard his knuckles turned white. Was he looking for something we didn't have? He asked her something else and I saw her shake her head again, her brows starting to furrow together. Kat wasn't happy about whatever it was he was asking for. By now every hair on the back of my neck was standing up.

The Man in Black, as I decided to call him, didn't like being denied. His jaw got so tight I worried he might lash out at her verbally. Maybe even physically. He glanced around the store at the other customers, some of whom were staring at him and Kat. Whatever he might do was going to have a lot of witnesses. He turned back to Kat, stared her down right through his sunglasses for a moment more, then stalked away, his lips pressed together in an angry line. He pushed his way rudely through clusters of customers in his effort to get to the exit.

Wizard hissed at him as he opened the front door. His head twisted at an angle to look up at the cat. His hands clenched into fists again as he stared down Kat's familiar the same way he had her. Wizard's ears plastered themselves to his head as a growl rumbled in his chest. I had never seen Wizard hiss or growl at anyone. Now even the hairs on my arms were standing up. For a second I wondered if the Man in Black was going to reach up and yank Wizard off the bookcase. He seemed angry not just at Kat, but at her familiar who was now crouched on all fours, fur fluffed out in all directions like he was ready for a fight.

Bandit crept over, adding his growls to Wizard's. Not that there was anything he could do, but he didn't like this guy either. The Man in Black tilted his head in my dog's direction. Could he sense Bandit?

I stepped toward them thinking I might have to head off a conflict between him and Wizard, but he turned and left the store, his hands still balled into fists. He almost ran into another man who wanted to come in. They looked at each other for a long second and I began to wonder if something was going to go down on the street, but the Man in Black stormed off. The other man's gaze lingered on his back for a few seconds before he turned back to the door.

I walked over to Kat and Pete, who were by the register, both a little pale. I heard the bell tinkle behind me.

"Are you guys alright?" I asked. I had never seen Kat look that shaken before.

"Yes, I'm fine," Kat replied, while Pete nodded his head.

"You sure? That guy was creepy. Wizard didn't like him at all."

"Yeah, me either," Kat said. "There's something dark about him. I hope he doesn't come back."

"Me either," Pete said. "He scared the hell out of me. There is something really off about that guy. I think he's crazy."

"I'm sorry you had to deal with him," Kat said, giving Pete a concerned look. She fished her wallet out of her purse, pulled out some bills, and handed them to Pete. "Why don't you do a lunch run? Burgers, sandwiches, tacos, whatever sounds good to you."

"Okay, sure," Pete said, taking the money. He smiled gratefully at Kat. I had the feeling he was relieved to be able to leave the store for a while. "I'll be back in a few."

"Take your time," Kat said. "No hurry."

I wanted to question her more about what had just happened, but the other man, the one who was nearly trampled by the Man in Black, approached the counter. Kat smiled when she saw him, although it wasn't the usual warm smile she gave those she knew and liked, or even to most strangers. This was the one I rarely saw, the one she gave to people she wasn't that keen on for whatever reason.

"Hello, Bruce," she said, sounding pleasant despite her tight smile. "What brings you in?"

"Just thought I would stop by and say hello since I've never been to your bookstore. Everyone raves about it, so I had to see it for myself."

The smile he gave Kat, then me, was the same one I saw on every car salesman, insurance salesman, or anyone trying to get you to buy or do something you didn't want to. He even looked like a salesman. His salt and pepper hair was smoothed to his head, not a strand out of place. His pink, Ralph Lauren button down shirt was ironed and starched to within an inch of its life, and his navy-blue slacks were too, the front crease jutting out like a shark fin. Brown, tasseled loafers rounded out his preppy looking outfit, which I had the distinct feeling was for show. Some instinct told me he chose his clothes more as camouflage rather than because they appealed to him. No wonder Kat didn't like him. He was as genuine as a forged Picasso.

"Bruce, this is Cami. Cami, this is Bruce Beauregard. He recently moved here. And joined my coven," she added, her smile getting tighter. For whatever reason, Kat didn't like this guy, this witch, being in her coven.

He stuck his hand out to me and said, "Pleased to meet you. Are you a native of Santa Theresa?"

Bruce's greyish blue eyes gazed at me intently, as if he was trying to look right inside my head. The hairs on the back of my neck tried to stand up again.

I reluctantly took his hand, and immediately regretted doing so for two reasons. The first was that he gave the kind of handshake I hated. Halfhearted, no real grip, no follow through. A handshake should always be firm, with commitment, and with at least two shakes. This guy gave up after half a shake, but held onto my hand. The second reason was that as soon as I touched him, I got the feeling of him being a disingenuous con artist more than ever. I wondered if he was going to leave a trail of slime on my hand.

"Not really," I said after I extricated my hand. I had to resist the urge to wipe it on my shirt. "Growing up I spent summers here, but that's it."

"How lovely. Have you settled here now?"

"No, just going to the U and working part time for Kat."

"I see. Well, you couldn't have a better employer," he said, turning his attention back to Kat. Her smile looked like it was nailed in place. "Or live in a nicer town. I only wish I had found it sooner."

"Is there something I can help you with, Bruce?" Kat asked, her smile fading fast.

"Nothing specific," he said, ratcheting his fake charm up a notch. "Although I have heard you have a marvelous collection of occult books here. I thought I might take a gander at those."

"They're at the back of the store," she said, pointing at the cases the Man in Black had searched. "Let me know if you'd like to look at anything. The cases are locked."

"Thank you," he said, giving us a last toothy smile before strolling off to browse our collection.

Kat let out her breath, then took in another as if to cleanse herself of bad vibes.

"What's the deal with Bruce?" I asked while I watched him out of the corner of my eye.

"He moved here about three months ago, and showed up at one of our coven meetings soon after that. I'm still not sure how he found us."

"And now he's part of your coven?"

"Yes," Kat said, her frown returning a little. "For some reason some of the other coven members were almost eager to have him join. I think they totally fell for his BS. I couldn't believe it. Normally we vet potential coven member thoroughly and take our time about letting them in. For him protocol was practically thrown out the window."

"I guess I'm not that surprised. He's kind of like a snake oil salesman. There have always been people that fall for their pitch hook, line, and sinker."

"I know, but I didn't think it would be anyone from my coven. I thought they were smarter than that."

"Do you think he influenced them in some way, maybe by magic?"

"I think it's a possibility, but even if he did, I can't prove it," Kat said, her brows now knitted together. "He has at least half the coven eating out of his hand now."

"You think he is going to try the same with you?" I asked, worry starting to brew in the pit of my stomach. I didn't want this guy trying to put some kind of whammy on my friend.

"He won't get very far with me," she said, pulling her gold necklace out of her shirt. A Celtic knot charm I had never seen before hung from it. "This is spelled to block any such magic or interference. I made it not long after he joined the coven."

I watched Bruce peruse the books.

"Is there anything you can do to help your coven members get free of his influence?"

"I'm not sure. It would be easier if I knew exactly what he did. If it really is just his charm that's won them over, they're going to wonder why I'm casting spells on them. Probably won't be too happy about it either. I'm going to have to find out more before I do anything."

"Good luck with that."

"Thanks," she said, a small smile tweaking the corner of her mouth.

"What did that other guy, the one dressed all in black, want?" I asked. "He seemed to be looking for something specific."

"The *Compendium Maleficium*. I told him we don't have one."

"That sounds like an ominous tome."

"It is. It's full of magic so dark it should never fall into the wrong hands."

"Did he ask you to find one for him?"

Kat took in another deep breath and let it out slowly.

"Yes. I told him I couldn't."

"Oh. Must be really rare, huh?"

"It is. I actually have a copy, but I don't keep it in the display. I'll never sell it. I'll never sell any copy I find. That book needs to come out of circulation permanently."

If Kat didn't want a book out there, it had to be bad.

"How many are there?" I asked, goosebumps sprouting on my skin. I was reaching my limit on weird for the day.

"There are three copies I know of. Mine, one rumored to be in a private collection back east, and another that could be anywhere. Its whereabouts are unknown. There could be more, I don't know. All I do know is that he wants one, badly."

"You have to wonder why. What does he want to do with it? Is he a witch too?"

"He's a practitioner of some kind, but he didn't have the feel of a witch or wiccan. Whatever kind he is, he's one that wants to get up to no good it seems."

"Hopefully you stopped him from that."

"Maybe. There are other books he can find that will give him at least some of what he's looking for. A guy as determined as he is will find one eventually."

"Well, at least he won't find it here. Maybe he'll leave Santa Theresa and go look somewhere else," I said, really hoping that would be the case. I didn't want this guy showing up again either.

"Maybe. Let's not worry about him anymore," Kat said, rotating her shoulders as if to shake off her ill feeling. "We have enough to keep us busy."

"Definitely."

"That's quite a collection you have there," Bruce said, sauntering up to the counter again. "It must have taken you some time to acquire it."

"I've been at it for a few years," Kat replied, only giving her smile a halfhearted attempt this time. "We have a lot of turnover though. We regularly send out books to customers who order online, and I try to add to our inventory when I can. Was there anything that interested you?"

"There are definitely some titles I will be mulling over," he said. "I assume you would be able to find something for me if I had a book in mind?"

"Possibly." Kat's eyes narrowed a little. "Is there something in particular you're looking for?"

"No, not right now. I just had a feeling, judging from what I saw back there, that you're good at finding rare titles others might not be able to. You seem to have a knack for it."

"Thanks. I just keep my ear to the ground."

"Well, ladies, I think I'm off," Bruce said, giving us another insincere smile and blast of his fake charm. "It was nice to meet you, Cami. Kat, I look forward to seeing you at the covenstead."

"See you," Kat said without any real enthusiasm.

"We've definitely had our fair share of weird customers today," I said, watching Bruce leave.

"No kidding. I hope that's the last of them," Kat replied before disappearing into the storeroom.

I went back to working on the display, but my mind kept wandering back to our unsettling customers. I glanced up at Wizard. He was back in his usual position, lounging indolently on top of the bookshelf so that he could survey everything in the store. Bandit was snoozing in a patch of sunshine by the front window. At least the animals weren't bothered anymore.

Pete came back with sandwiches looking like himself again. I ate mine while I finished up with what I was doing before the Man in Black came in.

"Hey, Kat, I didn't get a chance to ask earlier because it's been so busy, but could I get off a little early today? I have a date with Wynn."

"Of course! Another date, huh? Things are going well?"

"Well, they're not going badly, so I guess that's something. At least not yet."

Kat took my hands in hers and gave me a direct look.

"You need to stop being so hard on yourself. And be more optimistic. I have a good feeling about you two. Stop worrying. If he didn't like you, he wouldn't have asked you out again."

"Maybe, but he barely knows me. You know I'm an oddball, and not just because of you know what."

"You are *not* an oddball. You are special, in every way that's good. He's going to see that. He probably already does."

I sighed. "I hope so. I don't know why, but I like Wynn. There's something about him. I don't want to mess everything up."

"You won't. Just be yourself, and don't tell me that's not a good thing. It is. I know your mom sometimes makes you feel like you aren't doing anything right, but don't let her get to you. You're unique, and lovely, and if Wynn has half a brain he is going to realize that right away."

"Thanks. You're a good friend, Kat. I hope you know how much I appreciate you."

"Just as much as I appreciate you," she said, giving my hands a final squeeze.

"I just wish I could be as confident in me as you are."

"Well, if there was a spell for that I would cast it on you, but there's not. You're just going to have to accept that you have a lot to be confident about."

"I'll try."

I wished there really was a confidence spell. Finding it within myself was going to be a lot easier said than done. Especially by this evening.

Chapter 9

I t only took me a couple of wardrobe changes to get ready this time. I settled on a periwinkle and white sundress, with white, low heeled, strappy sandals. I left my hair down this time, although I made sure it looked neater than it usually did, and added a little blush to my make up routine. A little understated color on the cheeks never hurt, and I wanted to look nice for my date.

Wynn was prompt, knocking on my door almost exactly at 5:00. He looked nice in a pair of beige slacks, light blue dress shirt, and a dark blue dinner jacket. He had gotten a haircut, and now it was neat and combed back, not flopping over his forehead. Which meant I could see his lovely green eyes that much better.

"Hi," I said as I let him in.

"Hi," he replied. He came in and glanced around, taking in my living room.

White, overstuffed sofas and chairs took up the middle of the room, surrounding a glass coffee table that had a large clamshell filled with small succulents. Marine blue ceramic lamps with off white shades sat on matching glass end tables, and another lamp sat on the console table behind the couch alongside a small stack of books and a vase with an artfully cracked white glaze. Framed, black and white photographs of the California coast adorned the walls, and color photographs of my family sat on credenzas and other pieces of furniture that hugged the walls.

"This place is amazing," he said. "It's a Craftsman beach bungalow, right?"

"Right," I said. "You know your architecture."

"A little. I've always thought these places were beautiful. I'm amazed you found one to rent. I heard they're rarely available."

"Actually, this house belongs to my grandmother. It was my grandparent's beach house. They used to spend a lot of time here. After my grandpa died, she moved back to LA for a while, and then bought a house out in Palm Springs. She spends a lot of her time out there now. She lets me live here since I'm in college at UCST."

"That's nice of her," he said. "Did she do the decorating, or did you?"

"She did. She has an amazing sense of style. I didn't get that gene, unfortunately."

"Yeah, me either. I just pick functional things and hope they match," he said with a crooked smile. My knees felt watery again, like they did every time he smiled at me.

Just then Bandit trotted into the room and parked himself in front of Wynn. He peered up at my date, first tilting his head one way, then the other. I had to smother a smile while my dog tried to make up his mind about my human companion. Apparently satisfied, he got up and trotted back into my bedroom. Bandit was sometimes like Kat. He seemed to almost have a sixth sense about people.

"I'm going to grab a cardigan in case it's cold in the theater, and then we can get going. Feel free to look around."

Bandit was sitting on my bed with the doggy version of a smug expression.

"Do you approve?" I whispered as I grabbed my cardigan off the bed.

"Rowroo," he said, his mouth opening in a doggy grin.

"Good. I like him too. I'll be back in a few hours. Love you."

When I came back into the living room, Wynn was holding one of the pictures of my parents.

"Do you know Jennifer Tyler?" he asked, his eyes wide. "This is her, right?"

"Um, yeah. She's my mom, actually," I replied, hoping I wasn't going to be overshadowed by my mother yet again.

My mother started modeling when she was fourteen, and was one of the highest paid models in the world by the time she was sixteen. Hollywood came calling not long after that. At first she did commercials and small roles on tv shows. She was cast in her first movie at eighteen, made a few low budget beach bunny movies, and then cheesy horror movies before moving up to big budget, marquee studio films. It was while making one of those that she met my father. She was semi-retired now, happy just being a studio executive's wife. She liked socializing, throwing parties, and shopping better than long hours on a movie set.

"Seriously?" he said, his eyes widening. "Jennifer Tyler is your mom? No wonder you looked so familiar when I first met you. You look a lot like her."

"A little, I guess. My mom is the gorgeous, glamorous one in the family. I'm just the plain version of her. Other than similar features, though, we're nothing alike."

It was true. Other than blond hair, blue eyes, and similar features, my mom and I had almost nothing in common.

"Your mom may be the glamorous one, but you're not even close to plain. I like that you don't wear a lot of make-up. I can see the real you. And for what it's worth," he said, putting the picture back in its place and giving me a shy smile, "I think you're lovely."

"Thank you," I said, warmth spreading across my cheeks. His compliment made my tongue want to tie itself into knots again. The butterflies were doing summersaults in my belly again too.

Wynn escorted me to his car, an adorable mid-sixties, forest green convertible MG with whitewall tires and tan leather interior, and opened the passenger door for me. We drove farther down the beach to Schooner's, a quaint seafood restaurant that sat on the end of the pier, where he had made a reservation. One of the things I liked about Schooner's, besides the food, was that you could hear and feel the waves crash under you while you ate. And, of course, you had an amazing, unobstructed view of the ocean.

The hostess seated us at an outside table. Wynn held my chair for me, which caught me a little by surprise. My dad was one of the few men I knew that still did that. Wynn's mom raised a gentleman.

"So," he said as one of the staff filled our water glasses, "what was it like growing up with Jennifer Tyler as your mom? I assume you grew up in LA, right?"

"I did." I paused, thinking about how much I wanted to say about my mom. I didn't want to overshare about my problematic relationship with her, nor did I want to ramble on about her since Wynn had lost his mom. "My mom's not much different than other moms, except that people know who she is. In our neighborhood that doesn't matter much though. Pretty much everyone we live around is connected to Hollywood in one way or another. She isn't the only actress on the block. There is an Academy Award winner a few houses down."

Wynn leaned back in his chair, his eyes a little wide.

"Wow," he said. "I can't even imagine that. You must have had a really interesting childhood, growing up around famous people and living the Hollywood lifestyle."

My childhood had definitely been interesting, but not for the reasons he thought.

"It was a childhood. When you're a kid, you don't realize your life is any different than anyone else's. It's all you know. My mom semi-retired from show business after my brother was born, and she drove us to school and came to plays and whatnot just like any other mom. The housekeeper made our lunches though. My mom avoids the kitchen like the plague."

"Really? My mom loved to cook. And bake. Especially around the holidays."

"Yeah, not my mom. She has restaurants, bakeries, and caterers on speed dial. My mom always makes sure our housekeeper and other staff have holidays off to spend with their families, so food for our Thanksgivings and Christmases always comes from one her favorite restaurants, and the cookies and pastries from a bakery my brother and I love. Don't get me wrong, the food is great, but it's not homemade."

"As long as it tastes good, that's all that matters, right?"

"Right. Although it would have been fun to make Christmas cookies when we were little. I always wanted to make cut out sugar cookies and decorate them. Making a mess in the kitchen wasn't allowed though."

"You would have loved Christmas at our house. My mom and I made all sorts of cookies and pies. That's one of things I miss most about her." His got a faraway look for a moment, then he blinked.

"But, when you have your own family, you can bake those sugar cookies," he said, giving me that smile I liked.

"True," I said.

Our conversation was interrupted by our waiter, a young man in his early twenties who looked like he spent a lot of time on a surfboard. Medium blond hair with sun bleached highlights, a golden complexion, and a faint tan line along his wrist where his wetsuit ended were all a dead giveaway.

"Good evening, my name is Chase," he said while putting a basket of freshly baked sourdough rolls on our table. "I'll be your server tonight. Can I start you with any drinks or appetizers?"

We had been so immersed in conversation that we hadn't even looked at the menu yet.

"I'm fine with water," Wynn said. "Do you want anything else, some wine or anything?" he asked me.

"No, thank you."

The last thing I needed was wine going to my head. Just having a normal conversation sober was challenge enough for me. I didn't need to end up tipsy, which considering how little I drank, wouldn't take much.

"I think we need a little more time before we order," Wynn said.

"No problem," Chase said. "I'll give you a few more minutes."

After he wandered off to check on another table, I opened the menu. Tonight's special was grilled seabass. That sounded good, although I really loved the salmon here, and the clam chowder. I chewed on my lip, trying to decide.

Chase came back a few minutes later as promised, and I ordered the salmon and Wynn ordered fish and chips.

As Chase left, the soft rays of the lowering sun bathed my skin in evening warmth, and tinted the gentle waves of the ocean with hues of orange, yellow, and pink. One of the colors reminded me of the pajamas our date crashing spirit wore. I glanced around the restaurant, but I didn't see her anywhere. Hopefully she would stay away tonight. I wanted to enjoy my evening with Wynn without any more ghostly intrusions.

"Do you have any brothers and sisters?" I asked, resuming our conversation.

"No, I'm an only," Wynn replied.

"Oh, wow. Was that kind of lonely when you were growing up?"

"Not too much. My parents tried for more, but it didn't happen. I have a lot of cousins though, so it was kind of like having brothers and sisters."

"That's nice."

"What about you? Just the one brother?"

"Yep, my brother Jackson. He's five years older than I am."

"Does he live in LA?"

"Sure does. He's an entertainment lawyer. He works for the studio where my dad is an executive."

"Wow. So, your whole family is in the business?"

"Yes. I'm the odd one out."

"No interest in any of that?"

"None. I think my mom was hoping I would become an actress, but that never had any appeal to me. I don't even like having my picture taken. There is no way I would ever feel comfortable in front of a movie camera."

"That's okay. What you're doing is far more interesting anyway."

"Thanks," I said, smiling at him. I wished my mom felt that way. I also felt like I had talked enough about me. I wanted to know more about Wynn. "How much longer is your ER rotation?"

"A few more months, then I do surgery for a while."

"Are you looking forward to that?"

"Yes, although it's going to be a lot of hard work. It's a rotation I need though. Since I'm specializing in both medical and surgical oncology, I'm going to have to do surgery on my patients to do biopsies and remove tumors."

"You're doing two specialties? Isn't that more work, and more time?"

"A little, but it's worth it to me. I couldn't really decide which I wanted more because I really wanted to do both, and I figure this way my patients not only get more bang for their buck, but a doctor that can see them through more of the process. If I have a patient with breast cancer, for example, I can treat her with chemotherapy and do surgery if necessary without having to refer her to someone else for part of her treatment. A lot of times patients have to see more than one doctor if one kind of treatment doesn't work. I feel like it's better for the patient if they can stay with the same doctor for as much of the process as possible. I think it makes them more comfortable about their chance of survival, and helps build a better doctor, patient relationship."

"That's great. I don't think everyone gives that as much consideration as you have. Your patients are going to have a good doctor."

I was really impressed that Wynn was going through that much extra effort to make himself the best doctor he could be.

"Thanks, I hope so."

After Chase delivered our food, I found myself watching Wynn while we ate, taking in little details I hadn't noticed before. Strong hands with long fingers gripped his knife and fork, which he used in the European method like I did, not the American. His fingernails were neatly trimmed, and I could tell he made a real attempt at ironing his shirt. It wasn't perfect, but he had gotten the worst of the laundry wrinkles out. I had the feeling Wynn was the kind of person who, no matter how chaotic his life was, still tried to stay on top of things and did his best to keep his life orderly. Not an easy thing given the amount of time he had to spend at the hospital.

While we talked during dinner, I found myself enjoying his easy smile, the way his eyes became animated when he spoke passionately about something, his easygoing attitude about life in general, and his dedication to things that were important in his life. He had an innate kindness you didn't find in everyone, and I began to wonder if oncology was going to break his heart. An important thing for a doctor in a field like that was to be able to separate themselves from their patients in a way that would let them cope with the death of someone they couldn't save. If Wynn couldn't do that, every death would torture him, and he would either give up oncology, or his personality would change and he would become hardened just to cope. I didn't want either to happen to him. His empathy and compassion were some of the things I liked most about him.

When the check came, I reached for it since he had paid for dinner at Pietro's, but Wynn beat me to it.

"Let me get this," I said. "You paid for dinner the other night."

"That doesn't matter. I asked you out. It's on me."

"Listen, I'm not going to let you pay for every meal. It's not fair."

"I guess I'm just old fashioned," he replied, his half smile tweaking the corner of his mouth.

"While that's sweet, I insist on being able to pay for things too. I'm getting the movie tickets, and that's that."

"Okay," he said, relenting. "My mother would have given me an earful if she knew I let a girl pay for anything on a date."

"I know she raised a gentleman, but this is the twenty-first century. It's okay to let the girl pay for things," I said. "Besides, it would make me feel better."

"Well, part of being a gentleman is not arguing with a lady, so alright."

"Always wise," I said, smiling.

As we walked down the pier under the twilight moon, I found myself being happier than I had in a while. I was having a good time, and for once I felt like a potential relationship might not go sideways. Maybe Kat's sixth sense was right.

When we got to the theater, we picked a rom-com to watch since neither of us liked horror films or war movies, and the rom-com was the only other choice besides a kid movie. Wynn let me pay for the tickets and snacks as promised, and we sat toward the back of the dilapidated theater, which smelled of stale popcorn and spilled soda. My feet kept sticking to the floor as we shuffled down the aisle to our worn out, cloth covered seats that were dotted with stains I didn't even want to contemplate the origins of. It seemed like the floors hadn't been mopped since the theater opened sixty years ago.

"Maybe next time we should go to that fancy new theater that just opened," Wynn whispered as the trailer started. "The one with the restaurant in the lobby and the heated, reclining seats."

Santa Theresa had existed with just this one aging, independent theater, The Strand, for decades, but a regional chain had recently built a large multiplex across town in an area that was being developed for businesses and new neighborhoods. There were mixed feelings amongst the residents of Saint T about the development. Most of us liked our quaint little town the way it was, and weren't thrilled about a bunch of strip malls and cookie cutter home developments being thrown up almost overnight. There was talk of the mayor and members of the city council not being re-elected for allowing the development in the first place.

"Sure," I said, although I sort of felt like I was betraying the theater I had been going to since I was little. "It'll definitely be cleaner than here. It's such a shame the owners have let this place go. I think the padding in these chairs gave up the ghost about twenty years ago."

"I think you're right," said Wynn, giving me a lopsided grin. "I think I feel a spring poking me in the derriere."

"Maybe it's their attempt at 3D," I joked.

"Ha," he said.

The trailer ended and the theater's lights dimmed completely. I was suddenly much more aware of Wynn's proximity. I could smell his oatmeal infused shampoo, and I couldn't help notice that he was just as nice looking in profile. A nose as perfectly straight from the side as it was from the front perched over lips that were just shy of sensual, but were masculine at the same time. A chiseled, but not overly sharp jaw and strong, broad forehead framed a rectangular face that had boyish charm and displayed his amazing eyes like a jewelry pillow.

I found myself watching him almost as much as the movie. The movie was nothing special, but the more I got to know Wynn, the more I felt he was. A realization that brought a fair amount of anxiety with it. I knew I could lose my heart to someone like him, and if things went badly, my heart would break. I'd had my fair share of disappointment when it came to dates and relationships, but not much more than that. I'd always sort of thought no relationship would ever last long enough to get to the heartbreak point. My mother and Kat were the only ones with any optimism about my love life.

Wynn had put the bucket of popcorn between us so it would be easier to share. I ignored it for the most part because I was full from dinner, but when I reached into it absentmindedly halfway through the movie my hand brushed his. We exchanged a startled look, and I froze. I didn't know whether to take my hand out and let him get some popcorn, or just take some. He seemed to be gripped with the same indecision, so we just sat there for a minute, staring at each other. The movie seemed to fade away while I looked into those dazzling green eyes and relished the smoothness of his skin against mine.

Then Wynn blinked, withdrew his hand with a sheepish look, and said, "Ladies first."

I took some popcorn, but I couldn't have cared less about it at that point. My hand felt almost tingly where it had touched his, and the butterflies that always seemed to want to roost in my stomach were back. I could barely focus on the movie at all.

The movie ended about an hour later, delivering the expected happy ending, but I barely noticed. As we walked out of the theater, I could see Wynn glancing at me out of the corner of his eye.

"Did you like the movie?" he said.

"It was good." I couldn't have told you if it was good, bad, or indifferent, honestly. "Did you?"

"Sure. I mean, you know. It was a pretty standard rom-com."

"Yeah."

We stood in front of the theater awkwardly for a moment, neither of us knowing what to say.

"You want to get a milkshake or something at Woody's before we call it a night?" he asked. He was looking at me kind of like a kid giving his first book report, and I knew he was feeling as shy and unsure as I was.

"Okay."

Woody's, a malt shop that dated back to the 1950's, was about half a block down and across the street from the Strand. The décor—red vinyl covered booths, chairs, and counter stools, black and white checked flooring, vintage memorabilia on the walls, Wurlitzer jukebox in the corner— was all original. There was a Woodie— this one a wood paneled late '40's Ford station wagon— with the name of the restaurant painted on its doors parked out in front. Woody's had been in the same family since it opened and was a favorite of Santa Theresa locals.

'Donna,' by Richie Valens, was playing on the jukebox as we walked in. There were a few people at the counter eating hamburgers, tuna melts, onion rings, and other malt shop favorites. A couple of booths near the back were taken, but that was it.

Wynn ushered me over to one of the small round tables that sat between the booths that lined the walls and the counter.

"What flavor milkshake do you like?" he asked.

"Chocolate is my favorite, but I'm okay with anything."

"Are you okay with sharing one? I'm still a little full from dinner and popcorn."

Sharing one? A flush crept up my neck at the thought of sharing a milkshake with him, and the proximity to him it would bring.

"Sure, of course," I said, trying not to sound flustered. My nervousness was applying glue to my tongue again, and my stomach was doing flip-flops.

Wynn approached the counter. A teenage boy in a short sleeved, button-down white shirt, pressed white pants, black belt, and white paper hat took his order.

"Should be ready in a minute," Wynn said as he sat down across from me.

"The milkshakes here are great," I said while we waited. "My grandparents used to bring my brother and me here when we were little. We stayed with them for a few weeks in the summer. Sometimes it was my whole family, and other times just my brother and I would visit. This was one of our favorite places to come."

"It sounds like summers here were a lot of fun."

"They were. I've always liked it better here than in LA. The people are down to earth, the air is clean, and there's no traffic. It has a great beach town vibe."

"I kind of like that about it. I prefer small towns to big cities like Los Angeles or San Francisco."

"Me too. Where did you grow up?"

"Ramona. It's in inland San Diego County. My parents didn't like the hustle and bustle of big cities either, so they settled there and my dad commutes."

"Where does your dad work?"

"He works for the San Diego Zoo and Wild Animal Park. He studies the primates and some of the other animals there."

"That sounds amazing. I love animals. When I was little I wanted to be a vet, but I realized after a while it wasn't for me. I could never put any critter down."

"We love animals too. There's a whole menagerie at my house. We have four dogs, two cats, a potbellied pig, chickens, and two pygmy goats."

"Seriously? That sounds awesome. I love chickens. I always thought it would be fun to give them names like Agnes and Edna," I said.He grinned. "We have Henny, Penny, Dolores, and a rooster named Gus. Gus is a real character." He gave me a shy look. "Maybe one day you can meet them."

"I'd love that," I said, a delighted smile creeping across my face.

The jukebox was silent for a moment while it pulled another record from its inventory. Then, 'Only You,' by the Platters, drifted gently through the diner.

The boy in the white uniform dropped off our order, a single chocolate milkshake topped with whipped cream and a maraschino cherry, and two straws. We unwrapped our straws, which were the bendy kind, and slipped them into the milkshake.

Both of us leaned forward and took a sip, noses only inches apart. Our eyes met over the glass and I found myself blushing when I slurped up the smooth, creamy milkshake. I was suddenly self-conscious, as if Wynn was going to be able to see some weird flaw this close up. I knew I was being silly, but somehow I couldn't help myself.

I let the straw slip from between my lips and sat back a little. I was tempted to drink more, but I didn't want to seem like I was trying to wolf it down, and I knew drinking any more right now would give me brain freeze. Wynn took another small sip and gave me a bashful look.

"This really is good," he said as if searching for something to say.

"It can become an addiction pretty fast," I said, swirling my straw around a little. "The java chip is pretty amazing too."

"Maybe we can share that one next time," he said, his eyes lingering on mine.

"That would be nice."

I had an entire kaleidoscope of butterflies in my stomach now. This whole evening had gone much better than I could have hoped for. I leaned in for another sip. Wynn leaned in too, his nose only mere inches from mine. Being so close to him, smelling his shampoo, feeling his gaze on me made me flushed all over. The last slurp of the milkshake brought nothing but disappointment because I no longer had an excuse to be this near him.

Both of us reluctantly relinquished our straws, and Wynn took the glass back over to the counter to save the boy the trouble of collecting it.

"Are you ready to walk back to the theater?" he asked.

The hands of the black Felix the Cat clock over the soda fountain pointed at nine thirty. We had been out for four and a half hours.

"Sure," I said. Wynn pulled the chair out for me as I stood, then opened the door for me and escorted me onto the street.

While we strolled back, I found myself sneaking peeks up at him, wondering what he was thinking, or feeling. I would catch him glancing down at me at the same time, then flush a little and look away as if he was embarrassed. About a half a block away from the theater's parking lot his hand took mine. My breath caught in my throat when I felt his strong, smooth fingers wrap around mine as our palms met. I wished the walk back to his MG could have taken all night, but it was only minutes until we reached it.

He held onto my hand as he unlocked the door, then steadied me while I slid into the seat. Only when he closed the door did he let go.

I leaned my head against the headrest, my face tilted in Wynn's direction so I could watch him while we drove home. He would turn to me occasionally and smile when he saw me watching him. I was too happy to feel bashful. At that moment I couldn't think of anything I wanted to do more than memorize every detail of his profile.

I was so caught up in my dreamy fixation that I almost didn't see the ghost of the young woman walking stiffly down the street about two blocks east of Schooners. She had long, strawberry blond hair, freckles, and a vacant expression. Where was she going? I really wanted to know. In fact, I was becoming more convinced I *needed* to know.

I barely noticed when we pulled up to my house and Wynn opened the car for me. I climbed out, my head still filled with images of the ghost. Wynn walked me up to my porch, and said something to me that I totally missed in my distraction.

"Cami?"

"What? Sorry, I didn't hear you."

I wanted to kick myself. Thinking about the ghost could wait until later.

"I said I had a nice evening and that I'm glad we could go out."

"Oh yes, right," I said, my brain still having a hard time refocusing.

When I didn't say anything else, he said, "Well, then, I'll, um, let you get to bed. It's getting late."

He let his eyes slide from mine and took a step back. Did he think I was bored and wanted him to leave? Or that I didn't have a good time?

I reached out and caught his hand before he could step off my porch.

"I had a really great time tonight. In fact, I can't remember ever spending a more perfect evening. So, thank you for such a lovely date. I hope we can do it again soon."

A slow smile crept across his face as his eyes found mine again.

"Me too."

He took a step toward me, and after a moment's hesitation, leaned down and gently laid his lips on mine. I leaned into the kiss, finding courage somewhere inside me to press my mouth more firmly onto his and wrap my arms around his waist. His hands found the small of my back when I raised up a little on my toes so he didn't have to lean over as much. I was almost breathless as he gently broke it off. My lips tingled and my heart hammered while I stared into his glorious eyes.

For a minute neither of us said anything. It was as if the world around us had ceased to exist and there was only us, right now, in each other's arms. I could have stayed there, lost in a world of our own, but I knew our evening had to come to an end sometime. I lowered myself back onto my heels and slid my hands back until they were lightly touching the sides of his waist.

"Call you soon?" he asked as he stepped back and took one of my hands, lingering a moment on my porch.

"Okay," I replied, nodding.

"Have a good night."

He walked slowly back to his car, looking over his shoulder to make sure I had unlocked my door and was safely in my house. As he drove away I was giddy, delighted, almost dizzy. While I wanted to bask in those feelings all night, and hopefully have them permeate my dreams, I knew I had to shake them off. At least for now. I had a ghost to find, and not a lot of time to do it.

Chapter 10

I changed out of my dress and into jeans, a black, long-sleeved cotton shirt, and sneakers while Bandit looked at me curiously. He was expecting me to change into my jammies.

"C'mon, Bandit," I said, grabbing my car keys. "We're going ghost hunting."

Bandit's ears perked. Anything we did that wasn't our usual routine was fun to him. He liked adventure. He took his usual spot on the passenger seat and scanned the neighborhood while I drove back to where I had spotted the last ghost, the one with the strawberry blond hair.

The street was empty now, but I figured the ghost couldn't have gone that far. Since they all seemed to be heading north, I drove in that direction, occasionally making a right, then a left in order to be able to see farther to the east or west in case she had wandered down that way for a while.

It took about fifteen minutes of driving around, but I finally spotted her leaving what I referred to as the main part of Santa Theresa.

She was walking, in fact almost drifting at this point, uphill toward an upscale neighborhood that was built about fifteen years ago. I followed slowly behind her, hoping no one going by wondered why I was crawling up the street.

When she got to the top of the hill she banked right and made a bee line for a large house at the end of the road. I searched for the sign so I would know what street I was on. It was Colina del Arco Iris. She was going to the house on Rainbow Hill.

As far as I knew, the Rainbow Hill house never had anyone living in it. No one seemed to know who owned it. It was a large Cape Cod, but unlike others in the development, which were painted white with a bright blue trim, it was painted sepia with an espresso brown trim. It looked out of place in an otherwise bright and friendly neighborhood.

The street the house sat on was shrouded in dim, murky light. Only a few, scattered, arcing street lights hung over the pavement, their feeble glow casting only the dimmest of illumination. The one closest to the house was dark, its bulb missing. Its absence allowed an unnatural gloom to creep over the front lawn that reached all the way to the porch. There was no porch light on, nor any light on in the house. Its windows were dark, faded almost into the wood siding in the gloom. A chill crept over me after I slowed to a stop.

I parked about fifty yards away from the house and cut the engine and lights. I saw the ghost drift through the front door, which faced the street. It was so encased in shadow that I didn't see it until the ghost permeated it.

"Ready to investigate, Bandit?"

"Rowwwwwr."

Bandit seemed almost anxious, his tail lowered, eyes locked on the house. He had watched the ghost the entire time as well, and seemed almost more intent on finding out why she was here than I was.

We got out of the car and I glanced around the neighborhood again. I couldn't see anyone watching. I debated on whether to lock the car or not, but decided against it. It was a safe neighborhood, and there was nothing to steal in it anyway.

I crept toward the house, Bandit matching my pace in a border collie crouch. There weren't any other homes in close proximity— a big price tag bought you a large property and a fair amount of privacy— but I didn't want to draw attention to myself in case a neighbor happened to be star gazing or something.

When we got closer to the house a feeling of icy fingertips caressed my spine. Something was not right. The closer we got, the more a feeling of dread settled over me, and the more scared I got about what I might find. I wanted to know what was happening to these ghosts, but I now had the awful feeling that it was a lot worse than anything I imagined.

When I reached the house, I put my hand against the wood siding. Touching the house gave me the creeps even more. Like many of the houses in Santa Theresa, this house had interior shutters on the windows, not curtains or blinds, and every one of them was closed. You rarely saw houses with every shutter closed, even on the sunniest of days. I didn't know if there were any living people there, but there were definitely spirits. I could feel not only the one we had followed, but others. Their energy crawled across my skin like a cluster of tarantulas racing across my body.

They were *scared*. Their fear pinged on my nerves, almost grating on my ghost sense. What was going on in there?

I snuck around to the back side of the house to see if there were open shutters or any indications of activity. All the windows were shuttered on this side too, but there was one smallish window, almost level with the ground, that shone with a muted, yellow light. This house had a basement. I was shocked. Basements in California were almost unheard of. Some older houses, like my grandparents 1920's Craftsman beach house, had a large crawl space under the house, but no basement. I wondered if this was the deciding criteria for whoever had picked this house to get up to no good.

I stooped over and ran to the window, then got on my belly so I could get a good angle to see what was going on. Bandit combat crawled over next to me, his ghostly nose within a millimeter of the window. I could feel the cold, damp dirt through the thin, cotton fabric of my shirt. Its chill settled in right next to the icy fright that was growing in my chest.

"Be really quiet," I whispered to him. For some reason I felt it was important my dog not make any noise right now.

I nudged forward, peered through the window, and felt my stomach drop.

In the center of a rather large basement, in a space that had been cleared of stored personal things and miscellaneous junk, stood what I assumed from height and build was a man, his back to the window. He wore a long black cloak with a cowl. On the floor in front of him was a magic circle, made up of sigils I had never seen before, painted in red. At least I hoped it was paint, and not something else.

About three feet to the left of the circle a black candle sat on a silver saucer, its pulsating flame a murky red. Wispy, dark grey, oily looking smoke drifted up from the burning wick. I wondered what it was for. That candle and its foul smoke made my skin crawl. The light it cast offered little if any illumination. The main source of light in the room was the bare lightbulb at the end of an electrical cord that hung from the middle of the ceiling.

What my eyes were drawn to and didn't want to leave where all the ghosts crammed into the basement. They were young and old, male and female, from every walk of life. Every new spirit I had seen walking the streets of Santa Theresa, and Susan, the ghost from the hospital, was there. They were no longer dazed or confused. They knew what was going on down there, and whatever it was had them scared to death. They clung to each other, their gazes locked on the person who had forced them into this basement to await whatever fate he had planned for them.

Anxiety stirred in my belly. These were people that should have been able to cross over in peace like they were supposed to. Stopping them was wrong in every way. This man had no right to do that. What was he going to do to them?

He picked up a simple, unassuming silver bowl filled with something I couldn't identify from the small table next to him, ran his fingertips along the edge of the bowl, and began to chant, his voice rhythmic. I couldn't understand a word he was saying, but I knew I had to record this. I slipped my phone out of my pocket and started videoing.

At first nothing happened. Then the man's head, which had been bent down while he was chanting, swiveled in the direction of a group of ghosts huddled near a stack of boxes about fifteen feet away from the circle. Could he *see* the ghosts? Was he like me? His right arm, the one that was caressing the bowl, shot out and pointed at the spirits, his chanting taking on a commanding tone. One of the ghosts, a thirty-something woman dressed in jeans and a blouse who looked like she might have been a soccer mom when she had been plucked from life, began to cry.

"Please," she begged. "Don't make me go in there. I don't want to go in there!"

Despite her pleas, she was dragged into the circle. A shimmer began to form behind her, which became a long, dark, pulsating rift in the air that oozed some kind of black goo. Purple light the shade of faded bruises and rotting fungi bled through the rift, casting the circle and everything two feet around it in an ill begotten glow.

"NO!" screamed the woman as the rift began to swallow her up. "Nooooooo!!"

The other ghosts began to sob while they looked on in horror as the woman was sucked in through what I had to assume was a portal until all that remained, her hand still trying to grasp some kind of lifeline, disappeared too.

"Oh my god," I whispered under my breath. "Where did she go? What's on the other side of that?"

I steadied my shaking hands before I dropped my phone. It was time to get out of there. I didn't want to see any more ghosts go through that, especially since I couldn't do a thing about it.

I was about to belly crawl backward when a voice that made my ears want to bleed percolated out of the rift.

"Did you get the book?"

The man in the robe dropped to one knee, his head bowed.

"No, Master. The bookstore had no copies."

"Are you sure?" The voice grated in my ears like a metal sheet being dragged over gravel.

"Yes, Master. I searched the shelves. I questioned the witch who owns the store. She said she has no copies. She refused to help me find one. I will have to get one from another source."

The hammering of my heart made my chest tight. It was the Man in Black, the one who had given everyone the creeps! He was the one gathering the ghosts.

"She was lying. You said she had a copy."

"Perhaps she sold it, Master."

"Or perhaps she didn't want to sell it to *you*. We need that book. We are running out of time. The spirits, all the spirits must be transferred soon, or my chance to cross into your world will be lost. You must *hurry*."

The voice was angry, out of patience with its acolyte.

"Yes, Master. I will bring in more spirits. The spirit beacon,"— the cowled head nodded at the candle— "is working well. Spirits are drifting in daily. The tests with these ghosts are going well so far. The circle is holding. You will cross over, my master."

A face so hideous and misshapen I could barely look at it formed in the shimmer, its hateful gaze fixed on the kneeling man.

"For your sake, I hope so, Uriah. Maybe you should pay that witch another visit. Convince her to sell you her copy, or get you another one, any way you have to. Trying to find another one yourself will take too long."

"Yes, Master. I will get the book. By any means necessary."

"Don't disappoint me. Or I will make you pay."

"Yes, Ma—

"Rowwwrrrrrr."

Bandit! Despite my warning, Bandit was so irate over what he was seeing, he growled. The Man in Black's head swiveled around, searching for the source of the sound. My stomach clenched.

"Someone is watching us!" While the Man in Black didn't spot us, the apparition did. Its eyes zeroed right in on the window. "Stop them!"

The Man in Black bolted for the basement steps and launched himself upward at breakneck speed.

Oh. *Crap*.

"Let's go!" I whispered to Bandit frantically as I got to my feet and sprinted like my life depended on it. Right now, I was pretty sure it did.

My heart pounded while my feet propelled me across the dirt and grass. I wasn't out of shape, but I wasn't a track athlete either. I had to get around the house and back to my car before the Man in Black, whose name was apparently Uriah, made it upstairs and out the front door. Given his instant reaction in the basement and speed up the stairs, it was going to be close.

I rounded the corner of the house at a tilt in a desperate bid not to lose any speed, Bandit ten steps ahead of me and running like he was built to do this all day. I heard rapid footsteps in the house, and somehow managed to find another gear. I flew through the yard, my back itching and my shoulders tight while I waited for the sound of the front door flying open and the pounding of Uriah's feet when he thundered down the front steps.

My feet hit the asphalt of Colina del Arco Iris just as the front door was torn open so violently it sounded like it came off its hinges. A ball of ice blossomed in my stomach while I pelted down the street. I was six feet from my car when I heard Uriah's feet hit the pavement.

I pushed myself to my absolute limit, moving faster than I ever had in my life, but when I heard Uriah gaining on me, I wasn't sure it was going to be enough. He was going to catch me, his fingers snatching the back of my shirt while I tried to get in my car, pulling me back just at the brink of escape. I could almost feel his hands on me as I nearly collided with the side of my car and tore the door open.

I threw myself in, my trembling fingers barely able to pull the door closed. My hands were shaking so badly the key slipped past its slot twice. Finally, I fumbled the key into the ignition. I let out a whoosh of breath when the engine turned over. I pushed the gear shift into reverse, and jammed my foot down onto the accelerator.

Uriah's hand slammed on the hood just as my tires squealed and my car shot backwards. His murderous black eyes fixed on mine for one split second and I screamed when I nearly lost control of my Bronco as it rocketed downhill. I got a death grip on my steering wheel while I put as much distance as I could between me and Uriah.

Bandit whined beside me, his eyes fixed on back window.

I kept my eyes glued to my rear-view mirror while I raced backwards down the street. I needed to make sure I didn't run into anything in my desperate bid to flee from a dangerous practitioner and whatever he was worshiping down in that basement.

I saw the feeder street Colina del Arco Iris connected to and mashed the brake pedal, my tires squealing again as I did a half turn and pointed the car back toward Santa Theresa proper. My engine wheezed when I put my car in drive and slammed on the accelerator at the same time. The transmission groaned in protest, but it held together.

Houses on either side of me went by in a blur. I thanked my lucky stars it was late enough that the neighborhood was quiet and my chances of hitting anyone coming home from work were hopefully between slim and none.

When I got close to the main artery that led to the subdivision, I slowed down. Uriah was fast, but even he couldn't run forty miles an hour. I knew there was no way Uriah could have kept up with us, but I looked in my rear-view mirror anyway.

The street was empty.

I made a left and drove the rest of the way home at a pace that wasn't going to put flashers in my rearview mirror. The last thing I wanted right now was to get pulled over by a police officer. Me panting, sweating, and shaking was bound to raise all sorts of questions. Questions I had no sane sounding answers to.

When I got closer to my house, I broke out in a cold sweat all over again. Uriah saw me. He saw my car. He might have also seen my license plate, even in the gloom of the poorly lit street. If he had noticed me at the bookstore and remembered me, he knew where to find me. At least on evenings and weekends.

I pulled into my driveway hoping fervently that Uriah had been too occupied and arrogant to notice me at Beltane Books. If he hadn't, he would know how to catch up to me after all.

Chapter 11

I t was total chaos at the store the next morning even before it opened. Darla arrived at nine-thirty with her personal assistant to set up for her book signing. We opened at ten, but the line to meet Darla had already started forming much earlier, and it went up the block and wrapped around the corner. I was almost late because I had to drive several blocks up into a residential neighborhood just to find a place to park. The little lot I usually parked in was packed. Some cars were even wedged into places that weren't actual parking spots. There was a good chance their owners might get towed before they got their book signed.

I wanted to talk to Kat about what I saw the night before, but we were too busy helping customers, running boxes of books out to Darla as she depleted the ones under her table in record time, and refilling the displays of local goods. Not only was Pete in the store with us today, but so were some of the employees that worked during the day on weekdays. It was all hands on deck.

No matter how busy it got, my mind kept replaying what I saw in the basement over and over— Uriah on his knees, that awful face, that grating voice. My eyes flitted regularly over the big picture window that spread across the front of the store, worried Uriah might be standing on the other side of it, looking for me. I felt a constant itch between my shoulder blades all day as if there were eyes boring into my back. My gaze would dart to the window, but nothing. Just the long line of Darla's fans waiting patiently until they could enter the store.

Beltane had a legal limit of thirty people at a time, including employees, so everyone else had to wait outside. I was grateful for that limit because without it we wouldn't be able to move in here. And I wouldn't be able to spot Uriah if he slipped into the store and blended into the crowd. The last thing I needed was that guy sneaking up on me. Of course, it would be stupid for him to confront me in a crowded place, but that didn't mean my imagination wasn't working overtime.

I didn't get a chance to talk to Kat until we got the last fan out of the store. The book signing was supposed to end at three, but there were so many people waiting that it went past four o'clock. We sent Eve, one of the weekday employees, outside around one o'clock to keep anyone else from getting in line, but it still took Darla hours to meet and greet every fan. She never short changed anyone, no matter how tired she was.

After Darla and her assistant left, I let out a sigh of relief. Kat let Pete, Eve, and the other staff go home too, which just left her and me to close up.

"Cami, can you turn the sign to 'closed' and lock the door? We most likely aren't going to get any other customers, and I'm ready to call it a day. Anyone that wants something can come back tomorrow."

"Sure," I said, grateful we were closing early. My feet hurt from standing on them so long. I glanced around the store, taking note of the gaps in the shelves and the depleted displays. Darla's fans were like locusts. Many of them had bought far more than just a copy of her book. One woman had bought every other book Darla had written, some romances, soaps, honey, and pretty much one of everything else we offered. Pete had to help her carry all her stuff out to her car. It was a busier and more profitable day than even Kat had anticipated.

"Hey Kat, can I talk to you about something before we restock?" I asked as I slid onto the stool behind the counter next to hers.

"Forget restocking. I'm exhausted. You are too. The Monday crew can worry about that tomorrow morning." She stifled a yawn. "What do you want to talk to me about?"

"Actually, I want to show you something," I said.

"Oh," she said, her interest piqued. "What?"

"You remember when Deedee came by, and told me there were new spirits in town?"

"Sure. Have they been giving you trouble?"

"No, it's not that. But more have been coming, and I've been seeing them around town. I finally got to follow one last night."

Her eyebrows tented.

"Wait, you didn't go out with Wynn?"

"This was after."

"Oh, good. I was worried you canceled or something. I still want to hear about your date."

"I know," I said, giving her a tired smile. "Anyway, I followed one of the ghosts. All the way to Rainbow Hill. To the house at the top."

"That weird, brown Cape Cod? The one where no one ever seems to live?"

"That's the one."

"The ghost went there? Why? That seems like a strange place to go."

"This is why," I said, pulling my phone out of my pocket and calling up the video. I slid the phone over to Kat so she could watch it. She wouldn't be able to see the ghosts because phones couldn't capture their image, but she would be able to hear everything. She leaned over the counter, her eyes glued to the screen, eyebrows scrunched over them in concentration. As the events in the basement played out, the feeling of dread settled over me again.

I saw Kat flinch, and almost flinched myself, while that awful voice scraped through the phone's speaker. When the video neared the end, I heard my own voice telling Bandit to run as I fumbled with the phone. I had nearly dropped it in my desperation to high tail it back to my car.

"Blessed Mother, what on earth was that?" Kat half-whispered as the color drained from her face. "That Uriah, he's one the one who was here the other day, right? The one who wanted the *Compendium Maleficium.*"

"Yes, that's him. I think we now know what he wants it for."

"To bring whatever spoke in that awful voice into this world, clearly. What happened to the ghost you were following? Was that...did the voice crying out belong to it?"

"That ghost, and dozens of others, were all crowded into that basement. They were terrified. Uriah sacrificed a different spirit, not the one I followed, but he's sacrificed others, and he plans on doing the same with the rest."

"To bring that thing over?"

"Yes. I think he needs the energy of the spirits to do whatever ritual he has planned. Which he is still trying to fine tune, apparently. He has been testing his ritual and using spirits for that, but I don't think he has it quite right yet. Probably why he came looking for the *Compendium.*

He also needs more spirits. Right now he doesn't have enough, or that thing might already be here."

Kat closed her eyes and shuddered. "He has to be stopped. Those spirits deserve to find their peace, and whatever that was does not belong on our earthly plane."

"I agree, but I have no idea how to stop Uriah. Did you recognize what was on the floor? Or understand what he was saying?"

She opened her eyes again.

"Yes, it's a summoning circle of sorts. The symbols he drew on the floor are meant to help bring that specter over, maybe even contain it, I'm not sure. I'm not familiar with all the symbols he used. I didn't understand what he was saying. It sounded archaic, but I'm not sure what language it was."

"Hmmmm. I wonder why the summoning circle isn't enough. He was doing a ritual as well. Don't those two things go hand and hand? You would think that would be enough to achieve his ends."

"The circle may not be strong enough. Or, it may be acting as an anchor, and a containment unit for the entity, but he needs something in the *Compendium* to power it, or enhance it. Like a different ritual, or augmenting spell work. It's hard to say since I have no clue what ritual he's doing."

"I thought that's what the spirits are for, to power the circle," I said. It had seemed to me that spirits were needed to fuel whatever spell he was trying to cast.

"They may be simply what you said before, sacrifices. Dark magic often requires some kind of sacrifice. A life for a life. Or in this case, a spirit for a spirit. Only, this spirit, if that's what it is, is clearly much more powerful than a newly formed spirit. In order for it to cross over, enough spirits that equal his power must be given at the same time. I think that's why Uriah's gathering them."

"Then I guess the one I saw being sacrificed yesterday was definitely another test run. From what he said, and how the ghosts were acting, he has done it before. He might be trying to get a feel of the ritual, or find flaws in it, as well as test the stability of the circle. Maybe he's having to figure some of this out as he goes since he couldn't get the *Compendium*."

"So it would seem."

"That thing wants him to come back to convince you to give him the *Compendium*. I don't like that at all. You need to be careful."

"I'll tell him the same thing I told him before. I won't help him," she said. "He won't find anything here anyway. I don't keep the *Compendium* at the store. After seeing what he was doing, I'm more certain than ever a copy of that book should never fall into his hands."

She chewed on her lip for a moment.

"Something just occurred to me. They said they need more spirits to power this spell, to bring that entity over. So why are they here, in Santa Theresa, and not somewhere like Los Angeles or New Orleans? Places that are rife with ghosts. You've told me before that Santa Theresa is fairly low key in terms of ghostly activity. They seem to be making things a lot harder on themselves by having to drag ghosts here."

"I thought about that too. With the exception of a man that died in the University Hospital ER, and a woman in the ICU the other day, all the ghosts in the basement are from out of town, at least as far as I know. It would make much more sense for Uriah to do this in some big city where he has access to all the ghosts he needs. I think he *has* to do the spell here, because whatever he is trying to get here can only come over in Santa Theresa, for whatever reason. If he could do it anywhere else, he would."

"Okay, but why? Why is that thing tied to this town? And, is the house on Rainbow Hill important too in some way, or was that just convenient because it's always unoccupied?"

"I don't know," I said, wishing I had more answers. "Maybe there is some clue in the history of Santa Theresa. I don't know that much more about the history of Saint T than you read in guide books. I've learned a little more here and there from Chester and some of the others, but nothing that would shine a light on what's going on in that basement."

"We need to do some digging," Kat said, sliding off her stool. "The library has books I don't carry about the history of this area. We might find something there. But first, I'm going to call a fellow coven member. He's a history buff. If he doesn't have some idea of what this might be about, he can probably point us in the right direction so we don't have to go through every book in the library."

"That would be great. Not that I mind research, but between work and school I don't exactly have tons of free time to spend aimlessly searching."

"No kidding. Neither do I." She snaked her purse from under the counter. "Let's go back to my place. We can have dinner and talk some more. Right now, after seeing that, I want a glass of wine. Maybe a cocktail. Or a stiff drink. Yeah. A stiff drink is definitely the ticket."

"Okay," I said. I didn't want a stiff drink, but going over to Kat's place sounded better than going home. After everything that happened up on Rainbow Hill, I wanted company other than Bandit. Plus, with Kat's help, I might be able to find out what was going on. And maybe get a clue about how to do something about it.

Kat locked up the store, and I walked her to her car. She had actually managed to find a spot in the lot.

"Do you want me to drive you to your car?" she said.

"No. I'll—"

The ghost in the coral-colored pajamas that had been popping up and watching me, even talking to me, suddenly materialized in the parking lot behind Kat. She glared at me over my friend's shoulder, her eyebrows drawn tight together. What was her problem?

"Cami?" Kat followed my line of sight and looked over her shoulder. "Is everything okay?"

I let out a frustrated sigh.

"There's this ghost that's been following me around giving me the stink eye, and she just showed up behind you. She doesn't like me."

"Really? Has she said anything?"

"That night I had pizza with Wynn. She showed up at the restaurant and started giving me the third degree. I don't know what her problem is. I never get a chance to ask her anything. She disappears before I can."

"Is she still there?" Kat asked, glancing over her shoulder again.

"Yep."

"I'm guessing she's not one of these other ghosts."

"No. They all go straight to that Cape Cod. Her focus seems to be to annoy me."

"Well, at least she can't bother you at home."

"True. Thanks again for warding my house, by the way. The last thing I need is for her to show up there."

"My pleasure. Are you sure you don't want me to drive you to your car? I'd feel better about it."

"No, you head home. I'll be right behind you."

"Okay. See you in a few."

I turned my back on my ghost stalker and headed in the direction of where I'd parked my car. When she didn't catch up with me, I figured she had dissipated again. That suited me just fine. The last thing I needed was another confrontation with her, at least today. Having the events of the basement on my mind was enough. I'd worry about her another time.

Chapter 12

The walk back to my car had me almost as nervous as my flight from Rainbow Hill. Maybe I should have let Kat drive me to it. I shot a look over my shoulder every three steps, my head nervously swiveling back and forth, convinced Uriah was behind me.

He wasn't.

At least not that I could see. That didn't stop me from feeling completely unsettled. Or that spot between my shoulder blades from twinging.

I finally spotted my car after almost five minutes of walking. It was sitting alone now on the residential street where I had parked it. This morning I'd had to wedge it in between an SUV and a small pickup truck because every street had been crammed with cars.

I looked around, left and right, trying to see if anyone was lurking behind a nearby shrub or a shadowy spot between two houses, but I couldn't find anyone.

I hurried the last few paces and unlocked the car, sliding in and shutting the door as quickly as I could. I hit the door lock and felt the breath wheeze out of my chest. Bandit looked at me from his seat, his ears down and back. He was nervous too.

"I don't know what's going on around here, buddy," I said as I started the car. "But if there ever comes a time when you're in danger, you run, do you hear me? I don't want Uriah figuring out a way to use you like he did those ghosts in the basement."

Bandit whined and pawed at the seat.

"I can take care of myself, and there isn't going to be anything you can do to help me. I don't want anything to happen to you. I don't want to know what my life would be like without you," I said, my throat closing up a little. I *loved* my dog. He was my constant companion and the one thing in my life that never changed, and hopefully would never leave. I hoped that when the time came for me to cross over, that Bandit and I could leave this plane and move on to whatever awaited together. I didn't want Uriah or anyone else getting in the way of that.

I pulled up in front of Kat's house and killed the engine. She lived only a few minutes from downtown in one of the older neighborhoods of Santa Theresa. Her house was old, although it wasn't a Craftsman. It was a mid-century ranch, painted beige with a dark green trim.

"I ordered Chinese," she said when she let me in. "I hope that's okay. I'm dying for some Mongolian Beef right now."

"That's fine," I said. I loved Chinese food, as Kat well knew.

"I ordered Cashew Chicken and some other dishes you like too. And, I called a fellow witch, Greg, the history buff I told you about. I invited him over so we can chat him up about some Santa Theresa history. He should be here soon."

"Sounds good."

I knew Kat's coven was a big part of her life, although I'd never really met anyone in it yet. I'd seen a few when they'd come into the store, but that was about it. Kat tended to keep her spiritual life and her work life separate.

"So, how did your date go?" she asked while she opened a bottle of red wine. She tipped an empty glass at me, wanting to know if I wanted some, but I shook my head. I was still too jittery to enjoy wine. Or the bourbon that was sitting on the counter. Judging from the shot glass next to it, Kat took care of the stiff drink as soon as she got home.

"It was nice. We went to Schooners, then to The Strand for a movie. Woody's afterward for a milkshake. We talked a lot."

"Nice, huh?" she said, her eyes twinkling as she took a sip of wine. "So, no sparks flew?"

I found myself blushing when I thought back on my evening with Wynn.

"There were some sparks," I said. "He kissed me goodnight."

"Ooh!" She led me over to the living room where we plopped down on her overstuffed, forest green sofa set. I saw Wizard snoozing in his cat bed over in the corner of the room. I sank into the comfy cushions and got ready for some girl talk. "How was it? Scale of 1 to 10," she said, giving me a mischievous grin.

"A 9," I said, reliving the feel of his lips on mine. "Maybe even a 10."

"Really," she said, leaning forward a little, her eyes bright and fixed on me. "That good?"

"Yes. My knees got mushy, I felt swoony, the whole nine yards."

"You like him," she said, leaning back again. "I'm glad. I think he's exactly what you need."

"You do? Why?"

"Because you don't take care of you enough, of the inner you. You don't nurture your spirit enough, and I don't mean what leaves your body when you die. I mean that essential part of you that's the center of your happiness and wellbeing. You're a good person, with a big heart, but you give more to others than you do yourself. I think being with someone like Wynn, who's as kind and gentle a soul as you are, will be good for you. Good for both of you."

I thought about that for a moment. I was always reluctant to make connections with other people because of my oddness, particularly romantic connections. It wasn't that I didn't like people, I just found it hard to relate to them most of the time. Kat was my best living friend, and Deedee was my best non-living friend, but most other people in my life were acquaintances rather than friends. It was lonely sometimes, but I was used to that. That was why letting Wynn into my life scared me a little. He made me feel good, like I was worthwhile, and more normal than I usually did. I knew that if I got used to that feeling, that kind of happiness, it would devastate me if it ever went away. But, Kat was right. I tended to self-isolate too much, and being with someone like Wynn would be good for me.

"I hope so. He's sweet, and kind, and smart, and everything I could ever imagine or want. Sometimes I think he's almost too good to be true, like the other shoe has to drop sometime, you know?"

"I don't think there's another shoe to drop," she said. "I don't get a sense of anything duplicitous about him. He's everything you say he is. He's just right for you. You deserve him. So, get to know him. Enjoy yourself. Live a little."

I knew she was right. Getting to know Wynn better would be a good thing in my life. It might also get my mom off my case for a while. That in itself would be a huge bonus.

The doorbell rang.

"That's probably Greg," Kat said, getting off the sofa.

"Hey," she said as she opened the door. I could tell by how her shoulders shifted that there was something on the other side of the door she wasn't expecting. "Bruce. Hello again."

"Hi, Kat," I heard a man's voice say. It had to be Greg since it didn't sound like Bruce. "Bruce came over two minutes after you called." Kat stepped back and Greg, a shortish Asian guy with dark hair, a Hawaiian shirt, and cargo shorts walked in. He had an uncomfortable, apologetic look on his face. Bruce followed on his heels with his same air of confidence and aroma of BS he had at the store.

"Sorry to barge in, Kat," Bruce said. He had the same oily charm as the other day too. "When Greg said he was coming over for a visit, I couldn't say no to tagging along. I hope I'm not intruding."

I had the distinct feeling from the chagrined look Greg was giving Kat that he hadn't exactly asked Bruce to tag along. Bruce had basically invited himself along. I also had the feeling intruding was exactly what he had in mind. Why, I wasn't sure.

"Not at all," Kat said. "Please, have a seat."

She gave him a polite smile as she closed the door behind him.

Kat took her seat on the large sofa again, while Greg and Bruce sat down in the chairs that faced each other on opposite sides of the coffee table. Bruce was closest to me. He shifted, squinting at me a little. Bandit's ears flattened. He lowered his head and growled softly. My dog did not like Bruce. Neither did Wizard. He was awake now, eyes fixed on Kat's newest coven member, his ears flat, whiskers twitching.

"It's Cami, right?" Bruce asked, as if he was making sure he remembered my name correctly. "From the bookstore."

"Right," I said. Suddenly I wished he had sat where Greg was sitting. I didn't like having him this close to me.

"Cami, this is Greg," Kat said. "He teaches history at the University. Maybe you've had one of his classes."

"Actually, I haven't. It's nice to meet you though."

"Likewise. Kat's mentioned you before," Greg said, giving me a big smile. He seemed like a really amiable, laid-back guy. "It's nice to put a name to a face."

"She did? Hopefully she had good things to say," I said, although I knew Kat would never say anything bad about me.

"Only the best things. Said you're in the psych master's program at the U. Are you planning on being a counselor, going into practice?"

"I'm looking more at working within the criminal justice system, maybe as a profiler for law enforcement."

"Oh, wow. Well, whatever you do, I'm sure it will be exciting," he said, giving me a lighthearted grin. "So, Kat, what are you plying me with food about? You said you wanted to ask me some questions."

"I did," Kat said, her eyes sliding to Bruce briefly. The things we wanted to talk to Greg about we didn't want to share with Bruce. "Before I get into that, would either of you gentlemen like something to drink? Glass of wine? Soda?"

"I'll take a beer if you have it," Greg said, a twinkle in his eye as he winked at Kat.

"You know I always keep beer around for you," Kat said, smiling at him. "Modelo or Stella?"

"Surprise me," Greg said, settling into his chair.

"Okay. Bruce? Beer?"

"I'll go with wine, thank you," Bruce replied. He tried to appear as relaxed as Greg, but relaxed fit him about as well as long johns on a giraffe. Everything about him seemed like a well-crafted façade. I was as puzzled as Kat was as to why this guy was admitted into her coven.

Kat returned with the drinks. After she handed them to her guests, she sat down on the smaller sofa with me.

"Cami and I were brainstorming the other day and we thought it would be a great idea to improve the display at the store devoted entirely to the history of Santa Theresa. You know, expand on the inventory of titles I have now and make it into something eye-catching," Kat said, making up a story since we couldn't talk about what we really wanted. "Since you know the history here so well, I figured you could probably point us in the right direction of some good books I could order. Maybe some that are at the library so that I can have a look at them first before I invest in them."

"That's a good idea. I'd be glad to help," Greg said, taking a swig of his Modelo. "There's a lot more to Santa Theresa's history than most people know. Everyone knows about the Spanish settlers, the old Mission, and so forth, but there's a lot more, really interesting stuff. Particularly the time before the Spanish settlement. I can shoot you an email tomorrow with a list of books to check out. Was there any particular time period you're interested in?"

"Not a specific one. I'm looking for a broad perspective. And, anything that might be... unusual."

Kat's eyes flicked over to Bruce. I really wished he hadn't tagged along. I was beginning to like him less and less.

"You mean like a guide to Santa Theresa's haunted houses or something?" Greg asked.

"Santa Theresa doesn't have any haunted houses," I said, my mouth circumventing my brain yet again. I bit my lip. If there were haunted houses anywhere in town, I would have already known when I was a kid. They had a special vibration to them I couldn't miss. Regardless, I needed to stop blurting things out. "At least that's what my grandparents told me," I added lamely.

"Actually, they're right, unless you believe the rumors about the old Bothell house over on the east side," Greg said. There was nothing to the rumors about the little girl haunting the house where the Bothell family used to live. I had checked the house out when I was a teenager. It was run down and abandoned, but it was clean of ghosts. "But, Santa Theresa does have some interesting spiritual history."

"Really?" asked Bruce. He suddenly seemed much more interested in the conversation. "Such as?"

"Such as what's covered in the legends and accounts of some of the Native American tribes in this area," Greg replied. "Also, some goings on during the early settlement years, before and after the Spanish."

"Like what?" I asked.

"Back in those days there were accounts of spiritual disturbances in this area, of ghosts, and whatnot. The stories drew a group of supposed occultists to the area."

"Occultists?" I said.

"People who believe in the supernatural, like ghosts," Greg said. "They also believe in magic, which they attempt to manipulate the supernatural with."

"Not like witches do, but they do have their own practices. They're less well known," Bruce said with a smarmy smile.

"Right," said Greg. "There are a lot of books on the occult, as Kat knows, but they don't always cover practice and ritual. They just talk about occultism in general terms. Occult practices are often learned from fellow practitioners."

"Just like Wicca, in many cases," said Bruce.

"What happened to the occultists?" I asked.

"They moved on," Greg said. "Probably didn't find what they were looking for. At least that's what I read. Do you know any more about that, Bruce?"

"No," Bruce said, giving us all a disingenuous smile, one that didn't reach his eyes. They were cold, grey, and devoid of any emotion. If I'd had a Spidey-sense it would have been tingling in overdrive. "This is the first I've heard of them."

"Have there been any books written on those occultists?" asked Kat. The doorbell rang again. "That's our food. Why don't we continue our discussion in the dining room?"

Kat retrieved our food from the delivery person while I got plates and utensils out of her kitchen. I'd been to her house enough times that I knew where everything was.

After everyone dished up, Greg said, "There are a few that I know of. I have a book that covers a little of that subject that I'll lend you so you have one less thing to check out."

"Thanks, that would be great," Kat said, snatching up piece of Mongolian beef deftly with her chopsticks.

She was a master at using them, her fingers nimbly maneuvering the miniature staves to nab tasty morsels. I was a disaster when it came to using them. My fingers just couldn't seem to hold them properly, and eventually would spasm and send a piece of food sling shotting across the room. I stuck to forks. It seemed Bruce favored western utensils too. Only Greg was handling the disposable chopsticks as well as Kat.

"How much space are you thinking of devoting to this expansion you were mentioning?" asked Greg.

"Oh, I was thinking of moving the display to the front of the store, maybe even in the window," Kat said, embellishing the ruse. Although that wasn't our plan, it actually sounded like a good idea. "That way it will be visible to tourists who most likely will be the most interested in the subject."

"Can't wait to see it," Greg said.

"Me either," Bruce said, giving Kat another disingenuous smile. "Talking about all this makes me realize how little I know of Santa Theresa. I would love to learn more."

"It's a great town," Greg said. "I've been teaching at the U for over twenty years now, and I can't imagine living anywhere else. I plan on staying here even after I retire."

"It is great," said Kat. "I haven't been here as long as you, or Cami who's been coming since she was little, but it's home. I don't see myself leaving either, and not just because I have a business here. I love it here."

I found myself echoing their feelings about Santa Theresa. I had much happier memories here than I did in LA. Not only because there was less spiritual activity to be plagued by here, but because I felt a sense of peace and belonging that I didn't at home. I didn't know if my future was going to keep me in Santa Theresa, but I did know it would pain me to leave.

Our conversation shifted in other directions after we finished dinner, and by the time we were back in the living room Kat and Greg were telling Bruce about the Annual Food and Wine Festival that happened every September. Being a total foodie, it was one of my favorite events. I always ended up sampling way too many entries, and never could decide what to vote on, but I was stuffed and happy by the end of it.

"What are some of your favorite events, Cami?" Bruce asked. "You must have participated in everything by now."

"Pretty much. One of my favorites is the Chowder Tasting on the Pier. That's in October. Local restaurants and residents compete for top honors in that. Anyone can enter."

"Have you ever entered?" Greg asked.

"Me? No. I'm not much of a cook. I stick to simple things."

"Maybe Beltane Books should enter this year," Greg said to Kat. "I have a great recipe for clam chow-da if you need one," he said, chuckling.

"That might be fun," Kat said with a wicked twinkle in her eye. "I could serve it out of a big, black cauldron. Maybe wear a pointy black hat. It takes place pretty close to Halloween."

"Oh, I have to get in on this," said Greg, grinning. "I'm definitely helping out. I'll wear my Sorcerer's Apprentice hat."

"Deal," Kat said, grinning back. "We're going to own that chowder tasting. I hope your recipe calls for bacon. Every good chow-da needs bacon crumbles on top."

"You know it!"

Our evening came to an end around nine o'clock. Greg had an early class the next morning, and all of us were ready to call it a night. After Greg and Bruce left, Greg assuring Kat he would send her a detailed list of books the next day, I helped Kat clean up.

"It would have been nice to talk to Greg without having to filter everything," I said, collecting empty beer bottles and wine glasses, "but at least we got some information. We know there's been spiritual activity here. We just have to get that book from him so that we can narrow it down. Maybe it will have something specific."

"I hope so. That would make life a lot easier. Once we figure out what it is, we can do some more research on our own if we need to. I'll call Greg tomorrow and ask him about summoning circles. He knows more about those than I do. Right now he's the only one I want to loop into this. I'm not sure how many more of my fellow witches have fallen under Bruce's spell, and who else I can trust."

"Okay." I stifled a yawn. "I think I'm going to head home too. Thanks for dinner."

"Anytime. I'll let you know what Greg sends over."

"Sounds good."

I gave Kat a hug and drove home. I was feeling uneasy again, and wondering if Uriah had figured out who I was. Even though I didn't think Uriah knew where I lived, I made sure my doors and windows were locked.

Just in case.

Chapter 13

An insistent buzzing fractured a dream I was happy to be free of. In it Uriah was chasing me through a hedge maze, the creepy black candle from the basement clutched in one hand, and a wickedly sharp knife in the other. Around every turn and corner was a ghost I couldn't risk stopping to help. I knew if I tried, Uriah would catch me. I didn't want to find out what he would do if he did. The buzzing saved me from that revelation.

I cracked an eye open and peered blearily at my alarm clock. It was barely 6 am. Who was calling me this early?

I snaked my phone off my nightstand.

It was Kat.

My brain was having a hard time waking up. I blinked and tried to shake off my brain fog. Why was Kat calling me this early? Even if she wanted me to come in on my day off, she wouldn't call before the birds were even up.

"Hello? Kat?"

"Hi, Cami. I'm sorry to call so early."

Kat's voice was thick and rough, a sound usually born from crying and the buildup of more tears waiting to be shed. A bad feeling crept through my gut and rolled my stomach.

"Kat, what's wrong? What happened?"

"Greg's dead." Her voice broke and I heard soft sobs over the line.

The bad feeling coalesced into a giant knot, and settled in my belly like a brick.

"What? How? We just saw him last night."

"His house caught fire sometime during the night. He didn't make it out. They found his body when they finally put the flames out."

"Oh my god. Kat, I am so sorry. How did you find out?"

It was the crack of dawn. Had she gone to his house for something?

"I was his emergency contact," she said, snuffling. "Greg wasn't married, and we've known each other for a long time, so he listed me as the person to call in an emergency. The police notified me about twenty minutes ago." Her voice broke again. "I have to reach his sister and break the news. Then I have to tell the coven."

"What can I do to help? Do you want me to come over?"

"Thanks, but right now I have to get myself together and call Ann, his sister. I have to tell her he's dead, and hopefully convince her to bury Greg here in Santa Theresa. It's what he wanted."

"Okay, but if you need anything, call me. I can get out of class if you need me."

"Thanks, Cami. I appreciate it. There is one thing. Greg emailed a list of books last night after he got home. Guess he decided not to wait. I'm going to forward it to you so that you can look them up when you have time. The book he was going to lend us burned too, so we're going to have to figure things out without it. I hope you don't mind handling research alone while I deal with all of this."

"Of course not. You have more important things to take care of. I'll call you later and check on you, okay? And again, I'm so sorry."

"Thanks, Cami."

After we hung up I laid there for a while, staring at the ceiling. Greg was dead. Gone. My brain did not want to accept that fact. We'd just had dinner together. He was such a nice guy, and now he was dead because of a fluke fire. Sometimes I hated how the universe worked. Life could be really unfair.

"Rooooo."

Bandit was looking at me from the end of the bed, head cocked, eyes sad. Before he came into my life I'd had no idea that dogs could express emotion, especially something like concern. Or, maybe it was just Bandit. He was definitely unlike any other dog. Whatever the case, my dog emoted more than some people.

"I know, buddy. Kat lost a good friend. I wish there was something we could do for her."

"Rowr."

"I guess we'll just be her support team. Whatever she needs, we'll do for her."

"Rawrf."

"Glad you're on board with the program."

I debated whether to try and get another hour or so of sleep since my first class didn't start until nine. My chances of falling asleep again were pretty slim. Once I was awake, I was awake. Maybe I could put my time to good use. The U library opened at eight. I could do a little digging before class. At least then I would feel like I was doing something useful.

Chapter 14

O f all the buildings on campus, to me the library had the most presence, the most sense of history. It was one of the oldest buildings on campus, built when the university was established almost a hundred years ago. It was a stately structure, designed in the Beaux Arts style during an era when not only was there a level of craftsmanship that rarely existed today, but an attention to embellishment that almost no one bothered with now. I always felt a sense of reverence when I walked in.

Unlike many libraries which were tight, low-ceilinged buildings crammed with rows and rows of bookshelves and periodical displays, the U library was wide and open, with a huge vaulted ceiling, and the upper floors wrapping themselves along the perimeter of the structure. The ceiling was arched, lined with rows of rectangular windows that filtered in natural light. Old fashioned lamps sat on the many rows of tables and desks that filled the back half of the main floor, and early 20th century sconces dotted the walls to add to the library's illumination. It was by far my favorite place in the whole university.

I sat down at one of the computer terminals that was near the reference desk and logged in. The list Greg had given Kat had six books on it. It turned out the U library had three of them. I'd hoped to find all of them, but I was going to have to keep my fingers crossed the town library had the rest.

I took the stairs up to the third floor where historical nonfiction was shelved. The first book was about the history of the Spanish missions in California. While interesting, it didn't have anything noteworthy to say about the old mission in Santa Theresa, or anything special that had happened there. There was only a brief account of the priests that had run it, and the relationship they'd had with the local tribes. I put that book back.

The second book was a coffee table book, a look at Santa Theresa's history in pictures. There were photographs dating back all the way to the late 1800's, depicting life in Santa Theresa before the arrival of trains, cars, or anything industrial. Not that there was any large industry now. I perused the book for a while, staring at old black and white photos of buildings that were long gone, and others that were still standing, or pictures of long-ago residents of Santa Theresa, their expressions solemn and hardened by a life built on back breaking labor and sacrifice.

While that book was far more interesting, and I loved historical photos, I put that one back too.

The third book, however, had some promise. It was titled *California's Most Notorious Characters and Criminals,* and Santa Theresa and the surrounding area had several entries. There were the expected Depression era bootleggers and rumrunners— I wondered if the ones that had shot Chester were the ones mentioned in the book— along with a gang of bank robbers that had passed through town on their crime spree that had started in Los Angeles and reached as far as San Francisco.

The most interesting person mentioned was a priest named Father Raphael. He came to Mission Santa Theresa as a newly initiated priest, and soon made an impression as a man who worked hard in service of the mission, and for the people in its purview. Eventually he became the head of the mission, and that's when things got interesting. In autumn of that year Father Raphael gave last rights to a man set to be executed for heinous crimes. Days after that he was called to perform a mysterious rite on Rainbow Hill. He spoke little of the events of the night on Rainbow Hill, but as time went on, he began to rant that Santa Theresa was in the grip of a great evil. No evil ever appeared, and Father Raphael was eventually relieved of his duties and sent to another mission for confinement. He died there, still firmly believing that Santa Theresa was doomed.

There was no more information about Father Raphael, and nothing at all about the man who was executed, but I had a feeling in my gut that the events of that night had something to do with what was going on in that creepy Cape Cod on Rainbow Hill. But how was I going to find out what happened?

I searched the library's computer for any more information about Father Raphael, but there was nothing else useful. I also did a search for any books on occultist activity in the area, hoping to find the book Greg had mentioned he was going to lend us, but nothing came up. It was up to the public library now.

More students began wandering into the library to do research, and I realized it was almost nine am. I only had a few minutes to hoof it to my first class. I hurried out of the library, almost running into a cluster of undergrads.

"Watch it!"

"Sorry," I mumbled instinctively. My mother was not tolerant of a lack of manners.

I was in my seat seconds before my professor started lecturing, but I might as well not have even shown up. Every word he spoke went in one ear and out the other. All I could think about was the thing I had seen in the basement of the Cape Cod. The rite Father Raphael performed had to have something to do with what Uriah was trying to release. What other great evil could stem from Rainbow Hill? What else could Father Raphael have died ranting about?

The public library, a far less grandiose building than the U library, yielded two more books on Greg's list. The first was a book on some of Santa Theresa's most famous and influential residents, past and present. There weren't that many, so it was a short book. I scanned through it pretty quickly. There was a brief mention of Father Raphael, but nothing else useful.

The second book had no promise either. It was titled *The Paranormal History of California's Central Coast*, and was mostly a guide to haunted houses. There was nothing about spiritual activity in the Santa Theresa area, or about the evil Father Raphael had worried about.

I snapped the book shut in frustration. I felt like I was on a wild goose chase. Every lead I chased led to nothing useful, or only hinted at the information I wanted. The only real lead I had right now was Father Raphael, and the mysterious evil he had been obsessed with.

I decided to call it a day. It was almost four o'clock and I wanted to call Kat. Hopefully she had talked Greg's sister into having the funeral in Santa Theresa. If she had, her day had been more successful than mine.

Chapter 15

When I got home, I toed off my shoes and plopped on one of the couches in my living room. The tension in my shoulders felt like barbed wire was wrapped around my muscles and I just wanted to relax for a few minutes. Bandit made himself comfortable on the sofa next to me and put his chin on my lap. His soulful topaz eyes gazed up at me. He always knew when I was stressed out.

"Bummer of a day, buddy. Was hoping I was going to find out a lot more about what's going on."

"Rowr."

"Yep, that's what I say."

I had one of those moments I'd had so often since Bandit had shown up in my life where I wanted more than anything to be able to pet him. I wanted to feel his fur between my fingers, the warmth of him under my hand. But, it wasn't to be. At least not in this life.

I debated watching something on TV, but somehow that wasn't appealing. My brain was spinning in restless circles, churning over what I had read at the two libraries and mixing that in with the memories of the night I fled Rainbow Hill. What was going on up there had to be stopped, but I had no earthly idea how to do that. I knew nothing about magic, and there was no way I could help those spirits until I had some understanding of what was happening up there. Even then, I couldn't do a thing until they were free of the influence of Uriah's magic. The only person I knew who might be able to do something about that was Kat. I wondered how she was doing, and if she was even up for dealing with this situation anymore.

I fished my phone out of my pocket and dialed Kat. She answered on the second ring.

"Hi, Cami."

"Hi, Kat. How did everything go? Did you talk to Ann?"

"Yes. She's fine with the funeral being here, and she's letting me plan everything."

"Good. That will give you some closure."

"I suppose. Once I get over the shock that he's actually dead."

The sound of Kat snuffling and then blowing her nose echoed in my ear.

"I can't even imagine what you're going through right now. To lose a friend that way. He seemed like such a nice guy."

"He was one of the nicest people I've ever known. It's just so unfair. He was a great teacher, an amazing witch, and the kindest friend ever. I still can't believe he's gone."

"Listen, why don't you come over to my house for dinner? In fact, why don't you stay over for a few days? Being home alone right now is no good for you, especially since the last place you saw Greg is there."

"Actually, that sounds great. Thanks, Cami. You're right, being here right now is just reminding me of him. I'll throw some things in a bag and be over in a little while. Oh, before I forget, how did your day go? Did you manage any research?"

"Yes. Went to both libraries. Didn't yield as much as I hoped, but I did find out a little interesting information. I'll tell you about it when you get here."

"Okay. See you in a bit."

Kat was on my porch in less than a half an hour. She looked miserable. Her eyes were red rimmed and puffy, her complexion was paler than usual, and she seemed tired, like she'd had a really long day.

"Hey," I said, stepping back so that she could come in.

"Hey."

She had the handles of a leather overnight bag clutched in one hand, and a large pet carrier with Wizard in it in the other. Wizard peered out at me, his eyes like polished pennies embedded in pewter fur. His usual annoyed expression was absent, replaced by one that was inquisitive, like he was in tune to everything going on around him. Bandit trotted over and peered in through the grated door. Wizard blinked at Bandit and suddenly a muted purr like a tiny boat engine rumbled in the carrier. Bandit nosed the carrier and gave a little whine.

"I hope you don't mind that I brought Wizard," she said. "I don't like leaving my familiar with other people to take care of. And, I'd kind of like to have him around right now, you know?"

I knew exactly what she meant. Bandit had given me comfort more times than I could count. It seemed only natural that she would want her furry companion around too.

"Wizard is always welcome here. Come on, let's get you guys settled."

I led her to the larger of the two guest rooms. My grandmother had filled the room with vintage, Mission style furniture. A queen bed with a beautiful, burnished oak headboard sat against the far wall and was the focal point of the room. Matching nightstands on either side, a large dresser against the wall on left, and chair with slatted sides and leather seat cushions rounded out the ensemble. A large, colorful Amish quilt with a flower sampler pattern covered the bed, and a matching quilted throw pillow with one of the sampler flowers sat on the chair. Mission style lamps with amber, wood sectioned, pyramid shaped shades sat on the nightstands waiting to be turned on so they could fill the room with a beautiful, honey glow.

"Make yourselves comfortable," I said.

Kat put her bag on the floor by the end of the bed and Wizard's carrier on the quilt.

"Thank you so much, Cami. I really appreciate you letting us camp out here for a while."

When her eyes started to water again, I stepped forward and gave her a hug. I wished there was more that I could do to make her feel better.

"You're both welcome to stay here as long as you want," I said. "*Mi casa es su casa.*"

"You're the best, you know that?" she said, sniffling.

"So are you. C'mon. Let's go relax for a bit."

Kat let Wizard out of his carrier and the two of them and Bandit followed me into the living room.

"So, tell me about what you found," Kat said after she sat down on one of the overstuffed white chairs. Wizard hopped up into her lap and snuggled in as she began to absentmindedly pet him.

"In one of the books I found at the U there was a lot about a man named Father Raphael, who was the head of the mission back in the day, and some kind of evil he thought was in Santa Theresa. It talked about how he gave last rites to some prisoner, then did something on Rainbow Hill, and after that thought Santa Theresa was doomed."

"That's not strange at all," she said with a tinge of sarcasm.

"Right?" I said. "It's weird."

"You think this has something to do with what's going on up there?"

"It's a definite possibility. I mean, how many other things could be linked to Rainbow Hill? Santa Theresa has always been a quiet town. I've never heard of anything else that happened up there."

"Me either."

"Plus, Father Raphael was convinced that what he saw or knew about was dangerous. Whatever is up there now could end up being dangerous. Uriah has to do its dirty work for now, but who knows what it might be capable of once it crosses over."

"You mean it could actually achieve something real on its own here? Would it become partially corporeal?" Kat asked.

"I've never heard of a spirit becoming in any way corporeal, but that doesn't mean it can't affect this plane, even if it's not really part of it. Poltergeists do it all the time. I'm sure you've heard plenty of stories of people hearing banging noises in their otherwise empty house, or things suddenly falling off shelves with no explanation. I've seen malevolent or agitated spirits stacking and rearranging furniture, creating cold spots, and even appearing to people who wouldn't normally be able to see them. And those are just run of the mill spirits. Whatever that is, it's far from ordinary. I don't even want to guess what it could do."

"Goddess save us all from that. There's enough bad in the world already without that thing adding to it."

"No kidding. That's one of the things I love about Santa Theresa— it's peaceful and safe. I'll do anything I can to keep that from changing."

"Me too," she said. "So what now?"

"The Mission was one of the earliest settlements, so maybe digging into that might shed some light on this one criminal who's hanging Father Raphael oversaw after he gave the prisoner last rites."

"There might also be a public record of executions," Kat said. "Maybe at City Hall. We might also be able to do some digging into who owns the land that Rainbow Hill sits on, and who's tried to acquire it in the past. I have a friend that works in the Records Department. Maybe she can help us."

"That would be great." A lightbulb went off in my head, and I kicked myself for my brain not remembering this sooner. "You know, I just thought of something. The U library might have some old newspapers we could look through. There's an archive of vintage periodicals, and I'm pretty sure they have old copies of The Mission Gazette, the town's original newspaper, on microfilm. It was started right around the time Father Raphael was the head of the mission. The execution he presided over would have been reported on."

"We definitely need to look at those. When can we go?"

"I only have two classes tomorrow, one late morning and the other early afternoon. We could do the library before and City Hall after if you want."

"That works. I can have Eve open and close the store tomorrow. I'll check in while you're in class to make sure everything is going smoothly."

"Hopefully we can find something in those newspapers. I really want to know who was executed on Rainbow Hill."

"Me too," Kat said. "Maybe then we'll get a better idea of what that thing in the basement wants."

"The only thing I want is to figure out how to stop it, and Uriah."

"That makes two of us."

My phone rang suddenly and buzzed my butt. Wynn's name glowed on the screen. I wanted to answer, but I felt weird talking to him in front of Kat. I was about to decline the call when Kat said, "Is it Wynn?"

"Yes, but I can call him back later."

"What for? Answer it. It could be important."

I couldn't think of anything important Wynn could be calling me about, but I answered it.

"Hello?"

"Hi, Cami." Wynn's voice was hesitant, almost shy. "How are you?"

"Fine. You?"

"Great. What are you up to? Are you at work?"

"No. I'm at home. You?"

"Just getting off a little early from my shift at the hospital. I've been thinking about you all day, and I was wondering if you wanted to come over a little later, if you're available that is. I thought I would cook dinner for us."

"Oh. That sounds great, but I have a friend staying with me for a while." I glanced at Kat, who was smiling at me like she was my fairy godmother. "Maybe we could do it another time."

"Bring your friend. I'll see if my roommate can join us and we can make it a foursome."

"Hang on." I muted the phone. "Wynn wants to know if we want to come over and have dinner with him and his roommate. We don't have to. You probably don't want to, what with everything that's been going on. We can have a quiet evening at here."

"Are you kidding? And pass up a chance to meet Wynn? I don't mind. It might be a nice distraction from everything. Something normal in all this abnormal."

I realized she was right. We were both unsettled by Greg's death, and Kat was nursing her heartbreak. Sitting at home was only going to provide an opportunity for her to dwell on it.

I unmuted my phone.

"Okay, that sounds nice. What time should we be there?"

"Around six okay?"

"Sure. What can we bring?"

"Nothing other than an appetite. I'll text you my address."

"Alright. See you later."

"Bye."

I put my phone back in my pocket.

"We're on for dinner," I said.

"Good. It'll be fun."

Chapter 16

We arrived at Wynn's place, which was a ground floor condo a few miles from the beach and about ten minutes from my house, a few minutes after six. As I rang the doorbell, I had mixed feelings about having dinner with Wynn. Kat was still pale, and I worried our sadness was going to be a distraction and make Wynn feel bad somehow.

That feeling fluttered away when he opened the door.

"Hey there," he said, my favorite smile playing over his lovely mouth. "Glad you could make it."

He was wearing faded jeans, a green shirt which brought out his amazing eyes, and his feet were bare. Somehow, he was just perfect. I was suddenly really glad we had come. It felt good to be near him.

"Hi. Me too. Wynn, this is my friend Kat Howard," I said.

He stuck his hand out, which Kat shook. "Wynn Caldwell. It's nice to meet you. Please, come in."

Wynn's condo wasn't big, but it was cozy. The furniture looked a little worn— it was probably second hand— but it was clean, and the entire living room was tidy. I saw several gaming systems sitting in the entertainment cabinet under the tv— were there many guys in their twenties that didn't have an Xbox?— and iconic posters of The Clash, The Beatles, and The Rolling Stones were pinned to the walls.

"Can I get either of you something to drink?" Wynn asked. "Soda, wine, water?"

"I'm fine with water," I said.

"I'll take soda," Kat said. "Whatever kind you have."

"I'll get the drinks," said a man's voice from the kitchen, which was just to the left of the living room.

About a minute later a guy in his mid to late-twenties, who appeared to be a Pacific Islander, came out of the kitchen with two glasses. He handed one with water to me, and the other to Kat.

"Cami, Kat, this is my roommate Keoni Kamealoha. He's a medical intern at the U hospital too."

"Nice to meet you," I said.

"You too. I've heard a lot about you." He gave Wynn, who's cheeks suddenly looked pinker than before, a mischievous grin.

"Oh, really?" I said. "What all has he been saying?" I smiled at Wynn, whose expression became vaguely panicked.

"You know, how great you are, how pretty you are, how smart you are, that kind of thing."

"Okay, okay," Wynn said, with mock exasperation. "You keep trying to embarrass me and I'm going to have to tell the ladies that all the nurses call you 'The Hawaiian Hunk'."

I could definitely see how he'd gotten that nickname. Thick, short cut, wavy dark hair framed a handsome, oblong face, from which warm, brown eyes twinkled and a wide, sensual mouth expressed delight at making his friend uncomfortable. Broad shoulders, muscled arms and chest that strained his red t-shirt, and equally muscled legs encased in blue board shorts with a flower print made him look like he belonged in a male swimsuit calendar.

"Hey now," Keoni said, his grin getting wider. "If you do that, then I might have to let it slip that you're addicted to Looney Tunes."

"Okay, truce," Wynn said around an easygoing laugh. "Can't blame a guy for liking Foghorn Leghorn."

"Why don't you ladies have a seat," Keoni said, leading the way over to the sofas and two chairs. I sat next to Wynn on the larger sofa, while Kat and Keoni took the chairs that bookended the coffee table.

"So, you're in medicine too," I said to Keoni. "Is that how you guys met?"

Keoni nodded.

"We sat next to each other in anatomy class freshman year. Ended up taking a lot more classes together, studying together, and finally figured out that maybe moving out of the dorms and into a place together might be a good idea."

"Are you pursuing the same field as Wynn?" I asked.

"No. My field of focus is ER medicine."

"Ah. You want to be on the front lines."

"I do. You get to see all sorts of different kinds of cases, but you never have long term patients. It's always something new."

"I never thought of it that way. It'll never get boring, that's for sure."

"Exactly," he said. "Do you go to the U as well?" he asked Kat.

"No, I own Beltane Books in old downtown."

"Oh right, the place where Cami works. And where she and Wynn met." Keoni's mischievous grin was aimed at his roommate again. "That's how you guys know each other, huh?"

"Yes," she said. "Have you been in before?"

"No. Not much of a reader, except of course textbooks. I don't have time for more than that kind of reading these days."

"I'll bet. Where in Hawaii are you from?"

"Oahu. The North Shore. You been to Hawaii?"

"Not yet," she said. "I'd like to, though."

"You have to. It's the most beautiful place in the world."

Kat's eyes twinkled. "In that case, I'll definitely have to plan a trip. Can't doubt the word of the Hawaiian Hunk."

"No, you can't." He winked at her. "So, you ladies hungry? Baked potatoes are done, Hawaiian street corn is on the grill, and the steaks are ready to go on."

"That sounds great," I said.

"It does," said Kat. "Thanks for cooking."

We left the living room and meandered outside, except for Wynn who disappeared into the kitchen. Because they were on the ground floor, their condo had a fenced in patio off the living room, which was larger than the small balconies of the upstairs condos. A mid-sized propane grill sat on the far-left side, lid up. Corn still loosely wrapped in the husk crowded the right side of the grill. The mouth-watering aroma of its sweet and spicy seasoning wafted through the air.

Off to the right was a round, glass table with four white folding chairs surrounding it like a compass rose. Four place settings, plain white round plates and stainless steel silverware, were laid out. Wynn brought out a platter with steaks which sizzled when they hit the hot grill.

"Can we help with anything?" asked Kat.

"Everything's under control," Wynn said. "How do you like your steak cooked?"

"Somewhere in the neighborhood of medium," she said.

"Okay, I'll do my best," he said, a grin tweaking the corner of his mouth. "How about you, Cami?"

"Same. As long as it's not well done, or raw, I'll eat it however it turns out."

Keoni brought out a plate with four baked potatoes, and a dish of butter. Then he put on oven mitts and took the corn off the grill and shucked it. There was a reddish-brown seasoning that was sprinkled on the ears before the husks were replaced for cooking. As he put the plate of corn next to the potatoes, the aroma drifted toward me again. My stomach growled in anticipation. Once the steaks were done, Wynn put them on a small platter and squeezed it in next to the potatoes. There was barely room for our plates at this point.

"Alright everyone, let's eat," he said, holding out a chair for me. Keoni did the same for Kat.

Dinner was wonderful. It wasn't just the food, which was delicious, but the company was great. Keoni was a natural conversationalist, and kept the banter around the table easy going and fun. He shared anecdotes about some of the rounds he and Wynn made at the hospital, and got Kat to talk about when she first came to Santa Theresa, and about opening Beltane Books. There were parts to those stories I had never heard before. Kat was smiling, relaxed, and distracted, which was exactly what she needed.

"Wow, guys, dinner was amazing," Kat said. "I don't know what you did with that corn, but it was out of this world."

"Secret family recipe," Keoni said. "But, since you're a friend of Wynn's, I miiiiight be persuaded to share it."

"What kind of persuasion are we talking about?" asked Kat, a playful smile on her face I had never seen before.

"The easy kind. Come surfing with me," he said. "I'll bet you spend most of your time at your bookstore."

"Guilty," she said. "However, me trying to surf would be like an albatross trying to dance ballet. Total trainwreck."

Keoni laughed. "Don't worry, with me teaching you, you'll be a natural in no time."

"Um, I appreciate your confidence," she said, laughing too, "but somehow I don't see that happening. I'll just have to find another way to wheedle the recipe out of you."

"I'm open to suggestion."

Wynn was fighting a grin as he gave me a wide-eyed look across the table. "Cami, can you help me with dessert?"

"Sure."

I helped Wynn clear the table while Kat and Keoni went and sat in the living room. I had the suspicion that besides wanting to continue their conversation, they were trying to give me and Wynn some alone time.

I followed him into the kitchen with a stack of plates in my hands, silverware piled precariously on top. It was a small kitchen with a gas burning stove, sink, about six feet of corner counter and cabinets, and a fridge squeezed in by the entrance. His refrigerator, a vintage avocado green Sears Coldspot, had photographs and notes pinned on it with magnets that looked like fruits.

As I passed it on my way to the sink, one of the pictures caught my eye and I almost dropped the dishes. In it Wynn was standing at a viewpoint with Half Dome behind him. Standing next to him was a middle-aged woman I recognized as the ghost that had been following me around town. In the photo she wore jeans, a red shirt, and hiking books instead of the pajamas I saw her in every time, but it was her. The blood drained from my face like water down a sink. A wave of wooziness hit me.

Wynn noticed me staring at the photo.

"That's a picture of me and my mom while we were in Yosemite," he said. "That was one of our last family vacations. She got sick soon after that."

"You look a little like her," I said when I finally found my voice. My brain was still reeling.

"Mostly my smile and my hair," he said. That's why her mouth had looked so familiar. "And I kind of have her build, although I'm a lot taller."

"What was her name?" He probably thought it was a weird question, but I wanted to know what the ghost that was following me was called.

"Helen. Her name was Helen," Wynn said, his voice tinged with wistfulness. I gave myself a mental kick. I was going to make him sad if I wasn't careful. I tried to salvage the mood.

"You look like you were having a good time. I love Yosemite Valley. Did you guys camp?"

"We stayed in Curry Village in one of the tent cabins. Getting a spot at a campground in the park is nearly impossible. Have you camped there?"

"No," I said, putting the dishes in the sink while Wynn loaded the steak platter in the dishwasher. "My grandparents never took us, and my mom wouldn't camp if her life depended on it. We stayed at the lodge. She wanted to stay at the Ahwahnee Hotel, but it was booked. My mom won't stay anywhere that doesn't have electricity and hot running water. And a bathroom."

Wynn grinned. "Sounds like your mom doesn't like roughing it."

"My mom's idea of roughing it is sleeping on twenty-dollar sheets."

Wynn laughed. "How about you? Do you like camping?"

"I do. My grandpa liked to camp, so he and my grandmother would take my brother and me sometimes. Our last trip was to Big Sur. I was in high school. My grandpa died right after I graduated, so we never got another chance to go camping."

"Maybe one day we can go camping," he said, sneaking a glance toward the living room as he took my hand and pulled me toward him. Kat and Keoni were still talking and ignoring us. His green eyes fixed on me, his eyebrows tenting upwards a little. "You know, if you'd like to."

"That would be fun," I said. My stomach fluttered. First he had suggested meeting his chickens, and now he was inviting me to go camping. Did this mean we were officially dating?

"Thanks for coming over tonight on short notice," he said. "I really wanted to see you again, and with my schedule I never know when I'm going to have free time."

"Thanks for inviting me, and Kat. We both needed some fun tonight."

"Is everything okay?"

There was only so much I could tell Wynn, so I stuck to what was public knowledge.

"Her friend Greg died yesterday. They were close, and I didn't want her to be alone."

"Oh wow," Wynn said, casting a sad glance at Kat. "I'm sorry to hear that. You're a good friend."

"Thanks. She would do the same for me. Anyway, I'm glad we're here. That I'm here," I added, my cheeks getting warm. Admitting that had me in the grips of shyness again.

"Me too," he said. He pulled us farther into the small kitchen and out of the line of sight of the living room. His eyes roamed my face for a moment, then he leaned down and kissed me. His lips were warm and soft; they sent a tingle from my mouth all the way to my toes. I wrapped my arms around his waist to steady myself before my traitorous knees made me stumble. They got mushy every time we kissed.

"Hey, what happened to dessert?" Keoni called out. "Or did you guys eat it all yourselves?"

Wynn broke off the kiss with a grimace. "Be right there!" The corners of his eyes wrinkled as he smiled. "I guess we're being paged."

"Guess so. Do you need help?"

"If you could carry the plates and utensils, that would be great."

After giving me those, Wynn got a cheesecake with fresh strawberries and swirls of whipped cream on top out of the fridge. I followed him into the living room, anticipating a slice of one of my favorite desserts, but almost dropped the dishes for the second time that evening.

Sitting on the chair facing the kitchen was the ghost of Wynn's mother.

Chapter 17

I was rooted to the spot. Wynn was at the coffee table, waiting for the plates so he could serve the cheesecake, but I was frozen. The expression on his mother's face was angrier than ever. She was frowning so hard she practically had a unibrow.

"Cami?"

Wynn was giving me a quizzical look, and probably wondering why I had stopped dead in my tracks.

"Coming," I said, hurrying over so no one asked why I suddenly decided to imitate a statue. I put the plates on the coffee table and sat down on the sofa, hoping that if I ignored the ghost, she would go away.

No such luck.

Her fingers were drumming on the armrest and her glare was aimed pointedly at me. It took everything I had not to look at her, but the last thing I wanted to do was engage her right now.

Wynn handed me a plate with a slice of cheesecake on it, and a dessert fork, but my enthusiasm for luscious, creamy, cheesiness had vanished. My stomach was in knots. A lovely evening was on the verge of being ruined by an angry ghost.

"What do you think you're doing with my son?" she said. "Do you think you're in any way good enough for him?"

I closed my eyes and tried to pretend she wasn't there. I was going to have to treat her like background noise, otherwise there was no way I was going to get through this.

"Cami?"

Wynn had said something to me I had totally missed.

"Sorry, what?"

"I asked if you like the cheesecake, but you haven't even taken a bite. Everything okay?"

"Sure, of course." I swiped off a small chunk of cheesecake with my fork and put it in my mouth. "Mmm, yum."

I could barely swallow the luscious dessert. Its flavor made no impression on me at all. I might as well have been eating wet cardboard.

"Seriously," Helen continued. "Do you really think a girl like you is right for him? He needs a nice, normal girl. Not some weirdo who sees ghosts."

The second bite of cheesecake stuck in my throat and I almost choked.

"You know I'm right," she said. "I can see it on your face."

There was a part of me that felt that I wasn't right for Wynn, or for anyone, because of my weirdness, my connection to ghosts. Kat always convinced me I was wrong, which was why I had agreed to go out with Wynn in the first place. Now his mother was calling me out, making me feel more than ever like an outsider. I stared at my cheesecake. Who in their right mind would want their son with someone like me?

"Are you full?" Wynn was eyeing my mostly uneaten dessert. Kat was looking at me too, head tilted a little to one side. She raised her eyebrows at me and I darted a quick glance at the chair Wynn's mom was occupying. Her eyes followed mine, her eyebrows inching downward and toward each other. Probably wondering why I was glancing at an empty chair.

"Actually, I think I am," I said after I forced down the bite that got stuck. "I'm sorry. It's really good."

"That's okay."

He took my plate and put it on the coffee table. He leaned back against the sofa and slid his hand around mine. Normally I would have been thrilled by a gesture that said we were a couple, but I couldn't be happy with my stalker in the room.

"Ignoring me isn't going to change anything," Helen said. "You need to stay away from my son."

I stifled a sigh and tried to follow the conversation that was going on between Wynn, Keoni, and Kat.

"This is far from over," she said when I continued to ignore her. "Don't think for a minute I'm done with you. I'm not going to leave you alone until you leave my son alone."

She gave me one last glare and vanished.

Some of the tension that was thrumming along my shoulders and spine relaxed as she left, but the doldrums she had plunged me into remained. My own mother didn't approve of some of the things I did, and wished I was different than I was, but she loved me, in her way. Wynn's mother hated me. How was I going to be in a relationship with him with her haunting me all the time, and with her constant disapproval?

An hour later I still had no answer to that question.

"Want me to wrap the cheesecake up for you?" Wynn asked as Kat and I got ready to leave.

"Sure, thanks."

A minute later he handed me my dessert encased between a paper plate and plastic wrap.

"Call you later this week?" he said.

"Okay. Sounds good."

He gave me a quick kiss while our foursome said our goodbyes but I was too frustrated to even enjoy it. I trudged down the walkway behind Kat wondering what on earth I was going to do.

"Is everything alright?" Kat asked as we walked back to my car. "You didn't seem like yourself after dinner."

"My ghost stalker, the one from earlier, showed up in the living room."

"Seriously? What did she want?"

"She's Wynn's mom."

Kat's mouth dropped open like a drawbridge over a moat.

"Are you kidding? Wynn's *mom*?"

"Yes. There was a picture of her in the kitchen. Then we come into the living room, and there she is. Told me I'm not good enough for her son and that I should leave him alone."

Tears burned the back of my eyes and my stomach churned again.

"Oh, Sweetie, you can't listen to her. I don't know what would make her say that, but she's probably just a disgruntled ghost."

"Maybe, but she has a point. Wynn should be with a normal girl, not one with the issues I have. She's right. I am a ghost seeing weirdo."

"You listen to me, Camelia Rose Mitchell," Kat said. She stopped and put her hand on my arm to make sure I was listening. "You're not a weirdo. You are gifted. A gift she doesn't understand and you don't fully appreciate yet. One day you will, and you'll recognize why you were given your ability. As for Wynn Caldwell, he's lucky to have you. I'm pretty sure he's figured that out. Now you need to."

"Even if you're right, how am I supposed to continue seeing him with her popping up all the time and telling me how bad I am for him? She's already crashed two dates. One of these days he is going to notice something is weird because I get stressed when she's around. How am I supposed to explain why my behavior changes? He's going to think it has something to do with him, no matter what I say."

"I'm not sure, but we'll figure it out. Right after we do our research and figure out how we're going to help those ghosts in that basement."

I sighed. "That's definitely more important. I can handle one cranky ghost until we figure out how to help the others."

Right now the situation in the Cape Cod seemed easier to solve than the one with Wynn's mom. Ugh. Why couldn't my life ever be simple?

Chapter 18

The archives were located in the lowest level of the U library. A grad student, judging from the upper-level coursework he had sprawled all over the desk, was on duty. A plastic name tag pinned to his black t-shirt said his name was Hector. He peered at us over his wire rimmed glasses when we came in.

"Morning. Can I help you guys?"

He gave Kat the once over. At thirty-two she was a little older than most of the students that came into the archives to dig up obscure information for a class.

"I need to look at copies of the Mission Gazette," I said. "Specifically, the oldest ones you have. Are they still on microfilm or have they been digitized?"

Hector snorted.

"They're still on microfilm. I doubt anyone is going to digitize those anytime soon. I think you two are the only ones that have asked for those since I got assigned to this desk."

Hector disappeared down the aisle behind him. After rummaging around for a few minutes, he returned with a flat box filled with small film reels.

"Here you go," he said, laying the box on some of his paperwork. "These are the oldest copies of the Mission Gazette we have. I need your student ID until you return them."

I gave him my ID, which he slipped into a drawer by his waist, and picked up the box.

"The microfilm readers are in that room over there," he said, pointing to a doorway off to the left and back. "Do you know how to use one or do you need me to show you?"

"I've used one before, thanks."

I chose a machine close to the door and pulled over an extra chair for Kat to sit in. Then I scanned the film reels, looking for the one with the oldest copies of the Misson Gazette.

"Here we go." I threaded the film into the machine. "Let's see what's on this one."

Kat and I leaned over together, peering intently at the small newspaper script that scrolled by as I slowly turned the knob on the front of the machine. Page after page scrolled by, but there was nothing about any crimes or executions. After about a half an hour of searching Kat leaned back and rubbed the back of her neck.

"I think I'm getting eyestrain. I thought we would have found something by now."

"Me too," I said. "We're at 1825 right now, which is near the end of Father Raphael's tenure at the Mission. We have to be close. He was sent away right around this time."

I loaded the next microfilm and forced my tired eyes to continue scanning. I was beginning to think we were on a wild goose chase again when an article caught my attention.

"Wait, I think I found something." I leaned closer and started reading an article out loud. "'Ezekiel Blackmore, the infamous mass murderer who was tried and convicted of the bloodthirsty slaughter of over fifty innocent women and children, native and settler alike, finally met his end today. Apprehended several weeks ago by Sheriff Muldoon after a nearly six-month manhunt that spanned multiple counties, Mr. Blackmore was escorted by his captor and ten deputies to gallows built on Barlow Hill solely for his dispatchment to hell. Standing nearly seven feet tall and weighing over twenty-eight stone, special rope guaranteed to snap a neck the size of a tree trunk was provided by the hangman who oversaw the construction of the gallows. Father Raphael, whose attempts earlier in the day to provide last rights to the heinous Mr. Blackmore were met with unholy words and threats of damnation, presided over the hanging. No one from the public was permitted to attend, much to the dismay of those grieving murdered family members. The sheriff and Father Raphael have refused to disclose the eternal resting place of the murderer.'"

"That has to be who you read about," Kat said. "How many executions could Father Raphael have presided over on Rainbow Hill? This Barlow Hill they mentioned has to be the same place."

"I would think so. It was probably renamed at some point. Maybe because they didn't want a reminder of what happened up there, or wanted to draw public attention away from it."

I turned the knob a little to see if there was anything else, and found a charcoal portrait. Dread crept over me in sickening waves when it filled the center of the screen. Goosebumps erupted on my arms and my hands felt as clammy as a week-old fish as the memory of that hideous face came back to me. The features of the face in the portal had been muted somewhat by the pulsating purple light, but the eyes were those of Ezekiel Blackmore.

The artist had not only illustrated Ezekiel Blackmore's features, he had captured the profound murderous evil that lurked behind his eyes and was etched into every line of his face. I could hardly breathe while his face stared back at me from the screen of the microfilm machine. I was as certain of that as I had ever been about anything that Uriah was trying to bring over the spirit of the murderer that was hung on Barlow Hill.

"Blessed Mother," Kat whispered. Her eyes, wide with fright, were transfixed on the screen. "He hardly looks human."

"There wasn't any humanity in him. He was a murderer. Not only that, but the authorities wouldn't even execute him publicly. Eleven men guarded him until the noose broke his neck. What does that tell you?"

"That they were afraid of him. And, they were worried what else he might do if he escaped. He didn't just kill people, he slaughtered them. That's what the article said. Not killed. *Slaughtered*." She shuddered. "If only they had caught him sooner."

"It's a wonder they didn't. It's not so easy for a guy nearly seven feet tall and about four hundred pounds to blend in. He must have avoided towns and settlements until he went on a killing spree. They had to comb the countryside for him."

Kat forced herself to look at the drawing again.

"Is that the face you saw down in that basement? Is that what was talking to Uriah?"

"Yes, I would bet my life that's him."

"When was the hanging?" Kat asked.

I glanced at the microfilm again. "September 13, 1825."

"Today is the 11th," she said.

"That means the day after tomorrow is the anniversary of the hanging. And very likely the day Uriah wants to bring him over. That's why he's in such a hurry. He has to do it on that day. For whatever reason, Ezekiel can only cross over on the anniversary of his death. If Uriah can't do it then, he has to wait another year."

"Why on earth does Uriah want to bring him over? What purpose could it serve?"

"I don't know," I said. "There's nothing that I know of that Ezekiel could do for him, or to him. Then again, I have never seen a spirit remotely like this one. I also have no idea where that portal leads to and where Ezekiel exists now. All I know is that the ghosts trapped in that basement are terrified to go there. Wherever it is, it isn't good."

Kat shuddered again.

"That begging voice was heartbreaking. I need to figure out what kind of ritual they're doing. That's the only way we're going to stop it."

"Hopefully we can stop it soon. The thought of Uriah sending more ghosts over there is waking me up in the middle of the night. I need to help them."

"We will," she said.

I unwound the microfilm reel and put it back in the box.

"At least we know something about the spirit we're dealing with," I said after I stood up and grabbed the box. "It's more information than we had yesterday."

We went back out to the archive lobby where I traded Hector the box for my ID card, and then Kat and I left the library. I handed her my car keys.

"Do you want to head back to my place for a while? You can come get me after my classes are over and we can go over to City Hall and see what your friend can find."

"I might swing by the store for a while and check in. What time does your last class end?"

"Two o'clock. I can meet you at the lot we're parked in now."

"Okay." She gave me a half-smile and shook her head. "I almost feel like we're in the middle of a Nancy Drew mystery or something. Only darker than anything she had to solve."

"No kidding. Her mysteries seemed a lot more innocent in comparison. Wish ours was."

"Me too," Kat said. "Hopefully we'll turn up something else that will help unravel some of it."

"Yeah. See you at two."

As Kat left for the parking lot, I wondered again what we were going to do about Ezekiel. Dealing with him was going to be more complicated than dealing with an ordinary ghost. He was the spirit of a violent mass murderer. Based on what I saw in the basement, almost two hundred years as a ghost had done nothing to curb his violent tendencies. What was the thing Uriah was trying to bring over going to be like?

I didn't know, and I didn't want to.

Chapter 19

City Hall, another of Santa Theresa's stately buildings, dated back to the 1920's and had art deco flair around the entrance as well as around wall sconces and doorways. The records department was up on the third floor. We took the vintage elevator up, its beautiful art deco doors with inlaid suns made of alternating copper and bronze panels sliding open soundlessly and ushering us inside.

Kat had called her friend, Martha, and told her what we were looking for. Martha had already gotten together everything she could find on Rainbow Hill and was waiting for us. For a change we didn't have to dig through the material ourselves.

Martha, a petite woman with short, greyish hair who looked to be in her early fifties, was tapping away at her computer when we came in, her back to the door. When she heard our footsteps her head swiveled around, glasses with lenses so thick perched on her nose I wondered if she was one prescription away from being legally blind.

"Hi, Martha," Kat said. "It's good to see you. How have you been?"

"Hi, Kat. I'm well, thanks." Martha stood and joined us at the counter that separated the little foyer from her workspace. Papers and old photographs were piled neatly in the center. She patted it gently. "Pulled what I could find for you."

"Thanks. I really appreciate it. I hope it didn't take you too long."

"Not at all. It was actually interesting research." She separated the paperwork and the photographs, then slid one of the pages closer to us. "This is the earliest record we have of an owner for the land parcel that includes Rainbow Hill." Kat and I leaned over and peered at the aging document which was hand written in ink. "It was originally purchased by a man named Josephus Barlow in 1822. He paid about two cents an acre. Talk about a bargain."

That was three years before Ezekiel Blackmore was executed. Rainbow Hill had been privately owned at the time.

"Josephus Barlow," I said. "That's why it was called Barlow Hill back then, not Rainbow Hill."

"Exactly," Martha said. "Around 1825 there was some dispute over whether the parcel the Barlow's bought included Barlow Hill, now Rainbow Hill, or just the acreage to the west of it. Josephus Barlow claimed the land deed included the hill. The town claimed it didn't, even though everyone called it Barlow Hill. They said the land deed was drawn up incorrectly. For some reason the town didn't want the hill to be included, although why the hill was so important to them is unclear. It's just a hill."

Kat and I exchanged a glance. We knew exactly why the city didn't want to be included. They had a purpose for it. They wanted to hang Ezekiel on it.

"There was no reason given anywhere as to why the town wanted that particular hill?" Kat asked.

"Not that I could find," Martha said. "It's odd they would want that hill for anything when there was so much other land. Especially since legend has it the hill was cursed by one of the local tribes right after the first Spanish settlers got here."

"Really?" Kat said. "Why?"

"Supposedly because members of the tribe were killed on that hill by some of the Spanish. The tribe was living around there, and the Spanish tried to move them on. When the Indians resisted, the Spanish used force. There were casualties on both sides. The Spanish buried their dead on that hill after the Indians fled. The spiritual leader of the tribe cursed the hill so that those buried there couldn't move on to the afterlife. Their souls were doomed to be trapped there forever, or something like that. That's what we learned in a local history class I took while I was in community college."

The hair on the back of my neck prickled. The land was cursed to trap souls. Maybe that was why the town, and maybe Father Raphael, had wanted to bury Ezekiel Blackmore there, so that his soul would be contained forever. That way he couldn't get up to no good in the afterlife either. Maybe where he was trapped was a kind of purgatory for his spirit and those of the Spanish that were buried there. I wondered what had happened to their souls when Ezekiel joined them.

"Wow. I never heard about that," Kat said.

"Me either," I said.

"Most people your age haven't. They stopped teaching about that because the town council said there was no proof of that, and it made Santa Theresa look creepy," Martha said.

"That's interesting," I said, glancing at Kat. "So, the town fought Josephus Barlow for the land?" I asked Martha.

"Yes. The dispute continued for several years," Martha said.

Meanwhile they had hanged and buried Ezekiel Blackmore on that hill. I shuddered. If only the Barlows had known what they were fighting for.

"Josephus Barlow was finally able to convince a court he owned the hill in 1826." She showed us a court document that sided in Barlow's favor. "After that the family lived on the west side of the property until this." She shuffled the papers again. "The town decided it wasn't just going to take the hill back, but the whole property."

She slid another document over to us. This one had an official city seal on the top and was typed, not handwritten.

"The land was acquired from the Barlow family in 1898 in an Act of Eminent Domain, although there is no reason stated as to why. Normally a city, or county, will take land back in order to construct a railroad, highway, or something else for the public. Not in this case. They gave no reason as to why they wanted it."

That seemed strange to me. Why would they want the hill back after so much time? They had accomplished what they wanted to up there long before, and nothing strange seemed to have happened up there since. The Barlows had lived on a different part of the property. So why did the city still want the hill back so badly?

"Barlow's grandson, who owned it at that time, filed complaints, and even a lawsuit," Martha said as she shuffled a few more pages toward us, "as you can see here, but the city won and took back the land. They paid him for it, but they gave him pennies on the dollar. The land was worth far more than what they gave him."

"Wow," Kat said. "That couldn't have gone over well with him. The city sat on that land for almost a century. Then they up and sold it about fifteen years ago, right?"

"Right. It was sold for quite a lot of money to a corporation that develops both commercial properties and real estate." She presented us with another document. "A company called APEX Development. They paid close to twenty million dollars for that land. Then they built all the strip malls and housing tracts that are on there now."

"Are they the same company that built the new theater and what-not?" I asked.

"I don't think so," Martha said. "I remember a different name being attached to that. Sanderson, or something like that."

"The city made a lot of money on that sale. I mean, it took them a while, but it profited in the end."

"It sure did," Martha said. She lowered her voice a little. "Rumor at City Hall has it that the mayor has put the money in special fund, not in the city's bank account where it should have gone."

"What's he going to do with it?" I asked. I didn't know if there really was a curse attached to the land, but there definitely seemed to be corruption surrounding it.

"No one really knows. He campaigned on refurbishing Santa Theresa's aging schools and infrastructure, cleaning up and restoring the pier area so it can be designated a historical landmark, and things like that, so we'll see if he actually does that."

"Right. We'll see," Kat said. She glanced back down at the counter. "What are the photographs of? What the land looked like back then?"

"There are a few of the parcel which are just pictures of the land-scape, and not terribly interesting. These are photographs taken of the Barlow house not too long before the land was taken back, and another building that was on the property."

The house, a two-story blend of frontier and Victorian styles, wasn't particularly interesting. The other building, a large, rectangular structure, would have seemed just as unnoteworthy except for the strange things hanging around the wide, barn-like door. There were small animal skulls, birds' feet, and other things I couldn't quite make out. A circle with symbols in it was carved into the upper right-hand corner of it. It was too small for me to see much detail.

"What's all that?" I asked, pointing at the door in the picture.

Kat leaned over for a closer look. Her eyes widened for a moment.

"Not sure exactly," she said, her eyes flicking to Martha. "I'd have to look that up."

"This one," Martha said as she put an old black and white photograph on top of the papers, "is of Josephus Barlow's grandson, the one who had the land taken away. She flipped the photograph over for a second to read the neat, handwritten script on the back. "His name was Merrick Barlow. He's the one in the middle." She tapped on the photograph. "The others, I think, were men that worked for him."

I squinted at the central figure and my blood ran cold. The face that stared back at me had a resemblance that gave me chills.

"Um, does he look a little familiar to you?" I asked Kat. Her face was almost as pale as those of the spirits I had followed back to the Cape Cod.

She swallowed and nodded.

"He looks a lot like... Bruce. And the one to his left... he looks a little like Uriah."

My stomach churned when I looked at the picture again. She was right. Bruce and Uriah's ancestors had known each other. My mind began whirring. Was history repeating itself?

"Is there anything on who owns the house on Rainbow Hill?" Kat asked Martha.

"Um, yes," Martha said as she pulled a paper from the bottom of the pile. "Strangely enough, APEX Development still owns that house. It was never sold."

"Who owns APEX Development?" I asked.

Why would a development company hold on to one house in a neighborhood? What would they want with an empty house?

"The owner of APEX Development is Franklin Beauregard. Maybe he plans of moving into it."

Kat's complexion managed to lose what little color it had left. Hearing that name left me a little breathless as well.

"Yeah, maybe. Thanks, Martha." Kat mustered a shaky smile. "All this information is great. I really appreciate you doing this for us."

"Glad I could I help."

"I'll call you soon. We'll get together," Kat said as Martha gathered up the documents and photos into a neat pile again.

"Sounds good. Take care."

Neither of us said anything while the elevator took us back to the main floor. I was still trying to process what we learned. And what we saw.

"That man in the photo has to be Bruce's ancestor," I said, finally finding my voice when the elevator doors slid open. "It would be too much of a coincidence for him and Merrick Barlow to look that much alike."

"Definitely," Kat said in a voice barely above a whisper. "Bruce has history in this town. History he never mentioned. He acted like Santa Theresa was completely new to him."

"Maybe he doesn't know that much. The Barlow family was forced off the land. He could have come back recently to discover his roots."

"Maybe," Kat said. "But it can't be a coincidence that Bruce's last name is Beauregard. What do you want to bet Franklin Beauregard is his father? That means his family owns APEX Development and the Cape Cod on Rainbow Hill. They came back under a different name and bought back the land and built that house."

My stomach dropped like a broken elevator.

"The house on Rainbow Hill was probably built right on the sight of where Ezekiel Blackmore's gallows were. Or where he was buried." A million thoughts were flitting through my head. "So, is Bruce living there? Or hiding out there? He has to know what's going on in that basement. He must know Uriah. Which means..."

"Which means he's part of what's going on down there," Kat finished. "Uriah isn't acting on his own. He and Bruce are in this together."

"They have to be. Him owning that land and the house is too much of a coincidence. But why did he join your coven? Why is he pretending to be new here? Why not just hole himself up in that house with Uriah? No one would have been the wiser."

"I don't know, but there has to be some motive," Kat said. "I didn't want to say anything in front of Martha, but that symbol on the door of that building means that his ancestors were the occultists Greg mentioned. Maybe even practitioners of some kind."

"Do you think one of the real reasons the city wanted the land back was because Bruce and Uriah's families' were occultists?" I asked. "Maybe the local townspeople didn't like the idea of practitioners living up there. They could have decided after a while that they wanted to run them off."

"That's a distinct possibility. Back in those days anything that seemed like witchcraft or any pagan art was seen as black magic. I'm sure the town didn't want to be a haven for that."

"But what does that have to do with Bruce? That was all a long time ago. It's ancient history. Why come back here now?"

"I don't know," Kat said. "Maybe he wants revenge. Although there is no one left for him to get revenge on."

Clamminess spread across my skin as a though occurred to me.

"Maybe that's what the spirit of Ezekiel Blackmore is supposed to be for. He wants to use it against Santa Theresa."

"Why?" Kat asked. "Like you said, it's ancient history. The people that took his family's land are long dead. And, they got it back."

"Maybe it's the principle of the thing. Maybe the family is angry about being discriminated against."

"Okay, maybe. But how are they going to use Ezekiel for revenge? Could a spirit be used for that?"

"If you'd asked me a week ago I would have said no, but now I don't know. I have no idea what's in the *Compendium* they want so badly, or what kind of spirit Ezekiel is. But why else would they want him? There has to be a reason to summon a spirit. You don't do that kind of thing just for fun."

"No, you don't," Kat said. "Still, none of that explains what he wants with my coven. No matter how he has impressed some of my fellow witches, not one of them would ever participate in something like what he and Uriah are doing. They're all good people. Being a little gullible doesn't make you willing to do something like that."

"Oh my god." My stomach clenched so hard I could hardly breathe. "Do you think Bruce had something to do with Greg's death? He was the last person to see him alive. And, he was at Greg's house."

Kat's eyes shimmered with freshly made tears.

"Why would he kill Greg? What would he have to gain by that?"

"I'm not sure. He did seem awfully interested when our conversation turned to the supernatural. Maybe he didn't want Greg to help us. Maybe he was worried Greg might clue us in to what's up there."

"But why would he think we would even be interested in that? As far as he knows we're just interested in books."

"True. But…" My stomach roiled as a sudden realization hit me like a ton of bricks. "There is one thing he gained by Greg's death. Another spirit. The spirit of a witch."

Kat's eyes widened, and she put her hand on her stomach like she might be sick. "That means…"

"That means Greg is down in that basement. At Uriah's mercy."

A lone tear slid down Kat's cheek as we walked back to my car. "We have to help him. We can't let him be sent over to wherever that poor ghost went."

"We won't. We'll figure this out. If you can find out how to disrupt whatever ritual Uriah is trying to do, and break his hold over those ghosts, we can help them all."

"That's the problem though," she said. "Figuring that out. I thought Greg might be able to help, but he can't now. I have to find another source of information. I can't ask anyone else in the coven. They might say something to Bruce, and right now I want to keep my coven out of this."

"What about the *Compendium Maleficium*? You said you have a copy. There has to be something useful in it, otherwise Uriah wouldn't want it so badly."

She let out a shaky breath.

"We may have no choice. I really don't want to use that book for anything. I meant it when I said that book should be out of circulation, but you're right. There might be an answer in there. As long as I am not casting anything from it, I don't think it can do any harm. We're looking to undo something malevolent, not create it. Tomorrow we look at the *Compendium* and see what we can do to help Greg and the others. I want my friend out of that basement."

"Alright. Once we have that, we can visit that Cape Cod and put an end to all of this. Although this time during the day. I don't want to be up there at night again."

"I hear that. We just have to make sure the house is empty," she said.

"Not sure how we're going to do that."

"Me either. I might be able to find out where Bruce is, but we have no idea what Uriah might be up to."

"Let's look at your *Compendium* first and see if that even helps us. Then we can worry about everything else," I said.

"Okay," Kat said, taking a cleansing breath. "One thing at a time. I just hope we figure this out, and soon."

"Me too."

If we didn't, Santa Theresa could face the doom Father Raphael had been so worried about.

Chapter 20

Kat's muffled voice woke me at 2:30 in the morning. I was a light sleeper, so even her hushed tones roused me.

"Do you know when it happened?" I heard her ask as she padded into the living room. "She did? I'll have to thank her. When should I—?" I heard her feet again. It sounded like she was pacing. "Okay, thank you."

I pushed back my duvet and sat up. Bandit cocked his head curiously at me, then followed me out of the bedroom.

"Everything okay?" I asked, rubbing my right eye, which didn't seem to want to focus. Kat was in a pair of red cotton pajamas, clutching her phone tightly in her hand. Wizard was at her feet looking up at her, tail twitching.

"I'm sorry, I didn't mean to wake you," she said, letting out a deep, shaky, breath. "The police just called."

"Again? Do they have information about Greg?"

It occurred to me that the middle of the night would be a strange time for the police to be calling about that. I was clearly only half awake.

"Someone broke into my house. My neighbor, who suffers from bouts of insomnia, heard something and called them."

My sleepiness vanished, chased away by the cold chill that accompanied that revelation.

"Someone broke into your house. *Right after* Greg died in his. This can't be a coincidence."

"No, it can't." Kat ran her fingers through her bangs. "Whoever, and I think we can guess who, either wanted something, or they went there to kill me too."

"Maybe both. Ezekial told Uriah to get the *Compendium* from you any way he had to. I hope they didn't find it."

"They didn't. I don't keep it at my house. It's in a safety deposit box at my bank."

"That's good at least. They don't know that though. They probably figured they could break in to your house and scare you into giving it to them."

"And then maybe kill me and set my house on fire too. I don't imagine they would want to leave any witnesses behind to identify them."

A chill crawled down my back.

"Maybe. Although two people who know each other dying in house fires that close together might arouse suspicion. Not that the police would even know where to start investigating."

"They wouldn't. There is nothing to link Greg and me together except our friendship. We don't exactly advertise that we're witches, so they wouldn't know to take a closer look at the people in our coven.

Even if the police did start investigating, they probably wouldn't figure anything out until it's too late."

"Which means we need to get moving on the next part of our plan," I said. "If we don't, and they discover a way to finish that ritual, Ezekial is going to cross over, and those spirits in the basement are doomed. Literally. Whatever was on the other side of that rift seemed like some kind of hell."

"You're right. But first, I have to see what those jerks did to my house."

"I'm going with you."

"It's the middle of the night. You should go back to bed. I can take care of this."

"Are you kidding? I'm not letting you go there alone. Although are you sure you don't want to wait until morning?"

"The police are still there. I would rather go while they are, just in case. Uriah and Bruce will probably steer clear while there's a police presence."

"Good point. Let me throw on some clothes and we'll get going."

Two police cruisers were parked in front of Kat's house, their flashers silently splashing eerie blue and red blobs of light across the houses on either side of the street. One officer was standing by his car, hands on his utility belt. I parked my car behind his and cast a wary glance up and down the street. I was suddenly paranoid that Bruce and Uriah might be watching the house after all. I wished Bandit had come with us because he might have sensed something, but I had told him to stay home with Wizard.

Kat got out and approached the cop.

"Hi, Officer Birney," Kat said after glancing at his uniform shirt where his name was written. "I'm Kat Howard. This is my house. Are you the officer that called me?"

"No, ma'am. That was Officer Delray. He's waiting for you in the house."

"Okay, thanks."

I joined Kat on the sidewalk.

"Ready to go in?"

"I guess." She chewed on her lip, her brows furrowed.

"Are you okay? Do you need a minute?"

"I'm alright. I'm just..." She blew out a sigh. "I'm mad. And frustrated. I feel violated. Someone weasels their way into my house, then kills my friend, and then comes back to my house to do the same to me. My home is no longer my sanctum."

"I'm so sorry, Kat. I can't even imagine."

She sighed again.

"Might as well get this over with."

Officer Delray, a stocky, middle aged black man with salt and pepper hair peeking out under his cap, and a few extra pounds around his waist that were straining against his belt, stood just inside Kat's front door. He nodded at us as we entered.

"Evening, ladies. You Ms. Howard?" he said to Kat.

"That's me," she replied.

Her eyes flicked around her living room. From what I could see not much was disturbed. Some bookshelves were rifled through and an end table lamp was knocked over, but other than that the room looked the same as when I was over for dinner.

"Well, ma'am, it looks like they forced the back door to your kitchen. Probably with a crowbar. The kitchen seems untouched. They poked around a little in the living room. The back of the house is where they spent most of their time."

"Great," Kat said. "I guess I should go see what the damage is."

"Yes, ma'am. I'll wait out here."

I followed Kat to the back of the house where the bedrooms were, and almost bumped into her as she stopped dead in her tracks in the doorway to one of the spare rooms.

The room looked like a hurricane blew through it. A medium sized, round, wood table was flipped over, two of its legs snapped like broken toothpicks. The blue table cloth that had adorned it lay in a shredded heap a few feet away. Blue, white, and yellow candles were strewn in broken pieces all over the carpet. There were heel prints in some of the larger chunks. A silver bowl with a fist-shaped dent in its side was thrown in the far corner. Broken jars of dried herbs that had been smashed against the wall opposite the door littered the floor. Pages ripped from books were scattered around the room like leaves after a storm.

"Oh my god," I whispered.

"They destroyed my altar," Kat said. Her voice was shaking. "My herbs, my books on magic. Everything."

"But why? Bruce is a witch. Why would he do this? Shouldn't this be sacred to him?"

Kat looked over her shoulder at me, her eyes sad and angry at the same time.

"I don't think Bruce is a real witch. Given his family's history, I'm pretty sure he's a practitioner of some kind, but not Wiccan or witch. I think he's been pretending to be in order to infiltrate the coven."

"Could he do that?" I asked. "How could he be accepted into the coven if he's not a real witch?"

"He smooth talked his way in. I didn't want to admit him until he had gone through the rituals and proved himself, but I was overruled. Like I said before, he had some of my coven eating out of his hand in no time. We've never let anyone join us that fast."

"Okay, but what does he have to gain from joining a coven if he's not a witch?"

"I'm not sure, but there's obviously something he wants from us." She turned toward her bedroom. "Guess I need to see how bad it is in there."

Kat's bedroom wasn't destroyed, but it was close enough. It was thoroughly tossed. Sheets, blankets, and pillows were strewn on the floor, and her mattress was tilted over the edge of the bed like a listing ship. Her bookshelf was tipped over, now face down on the floor like a drunk after a bender. Some of the books had escaped like rats leaving a sinking ship and were strewn across the floor. The drawers of her dresser stuck out at awkward angles, the clothes spilling out like candle wax. Even the paintings on her wall hung off kilter like mountain climbers that were clinging on by one hand, desperate not to plummet to their death.

What covered most of the floor was the contents of Kat's closet. Clothing and broken hangers dotted the room in messy heaps, shoes were scattered like jacks in a child's game, and her blue, Samsonite hardcover suitcase lay open and misshapen in the center of the room. Either it had been thrown violently, or someone had taken out their frustration and twisted it along the hinges in a fit of rage. Either way, it was never going to close again.

The mess continued inside the closet where storage boxes lay on their sides, their contents rifled through and tossed aside while the intruders hunted for the *Compendium*.

"Wow," I said. "They really went to town in here."

"No kidding. They did their best to destroy as much as they could."

"They were frustrated they couldn't get their hands on the *Compendium*."

"They got their hands on everything else." Kat's eyes shimmered with unshed tears as she surveyed her violated bedroom.

"I'm so sorry, Kat. I'll help you clean it all up."

"Thanks, Cami." Kat swiped an escaping tear from her cheek. "I'll deal with all of this later. I don't even want to be here right now."

We thanked officer Delray and I drove us home, my eyes on my rear-view mirror to see if we had a tail. What if Uriah or Bruce had been lurking near the house after all? They might have waited for us to show up so they could follow us home and finish the job. And even if they didn't risk that, what if they had been searching for my address? Did Bruce know my last name? As far as I knew he didn't, but who knew where he had been digging? It wasn't hard to find information if you knew where to look.

I took an indirect route home, turning down random streets just in case. I couldn't see anyone following us, but I wasn't taking any chances.

Chapter 21

We were at the bank promptly at 9 am. A middle-aged woman in a navy pant suit led us to the safety deposit vault. It was a large, square room with rows of safety deposit boxes in all sizes from floor to ceiling on three walls, and a wall made up of bars through which we entered. After Kat used her key to unlock her box, the bank assistant pulled it from its slot and led us out of the deposit box room to a small adjoining room with a square table and two chairs.

"When you're done, push the red buzzer by the door," the bank woman said after she put the deposit box on the table. "I'll return your box for you."

"Thank you," Kat said before the woman closed the door to the little room.

Kat frowned at the safety deposit box and rubbed her arms.

"Are you okay?" I asked.

"Yes," Kat said, her brow still furrowed. "I just hate that book. Touching it always disturbs me."

"Are you okay to do this?"

"Yes." Kat took in a deep breath in through her nose, and let it slowly pass her lips. "I'll be fine."

Her hand rested a moment on the lid of the box, then lifted it to reveal some documents and several small, black, felt covered boxes I suspected held jewelry. Sitting on top of the small pile of papers was a leatherbound book. Since Kat told me about the *Compendium*, I'd had every image of every creepy magic book I had ever seen in any movie or read about in novels going through my head. They were always thick, filled with tattered edged, often yellow pages, covered in worn leather, and had some kind of glyph or rune on the cover. The *Compendium* Kat had was just like that. It had a symbol I didn't recognize embossed on the front of the dark brown leather cover and two, silver, hinged clasps near the top and bottom corners of the book. I couldn't tell yet whether the pages were white or not, but the edges were uneven.

Kat rubbed her hands on her jeans and stared at the *Compendium*. She took a deep breath in again and blew it out slowly. Her hands still didn't move toward the book.

"Do you want me to take it out? If you don't want to touch it, I can leaf through it and you can just do the reading," I said.

"No, it's best if you don't touch it."

"Why? I'm not a witch, so it shouldn't have the same effect on me, right?"

"I wouldn't count on it. You're sensitive. Highly sensitive actually. That's what allows you to see spirits. People like you are rare. Not only could you be affected by the book, but it might find something in you it likes. Best not to risk it."

"You talk about it like it's alive."

"It feels that way sometimes. There is definitely energy in this book. Sometimes I wonder if some kind of presence is trapped in it."

"Like what?" I asked.

"Like the psychic imprint of the practitioner who created this book, or something they called up. Whatever part of themselves, or it, they imbued on this book. Whoever it was definitely had an affinity for the dark side of magic. It wouldn't surprise me if they believed in demons and were hell bent on summoning one. Or something like Ezekiel."

"They couldn't have been successful, right? We would know if there was some evil presence like that roaming the earth. There would be chaos everywhere."

"Would we? Watch the news sometime. It can be argued there is evil influence everywhere. Something like Ezekiel could be guiding, maybe even controlling, anyone, possibly without their knowledge. I don't think there are demons in the classical sense, or that something like them is roaming the earth, but you of all people know there are spirits in this realm. You also know not all of them are good. Who knows what the really strong and malevolent ones can get up to."

She was right, I did know. I had encountered more than a few malevolent ghosts over the years, some of which had wanted me to do things for them. I brushed them off and ignored them, sometimes ran from them, but someone who was mildly sensitive, but who couldn't actually see ghosts might still be affected by one. They would think the ideas the spirit was whispering in their ear were their own.

My stomach gave a queasy hitch.

"Let's hope most people aren't sensitive enough for that," I said.

"It only takes a few in the right positions of power." She rubbed her hands on her jeans again. "Okay, let's get this over with."

She reached into the box and took out the book. She grimaced as her fingers touched the leather, a grimace that didn't go away after she put the book on the table.

"Can I ask you something?"

"Of course," she said, glancing at me for a moment, eyebrows tented.

"You've said this book is practically evil, and shouldn't fall into the hands of anyone like Uriah. In fact, you don't want anyone to have it. So...why haven't you destroyed it? I mean, wouldn't the world be better off without it?"

"I want to, believe me. I just...can't. For some reason I can't bring myself to do it. Every time I try, I can't follow through."

"The book is influencing you?"

"Not in everyday life, thank the Goddess, but it seems to have an effect on me every time I try to get rid of it."

"It wants to stay in this world."

"It sure does." She sighed. "Right now, its will is stronger than mine."

"There has to be a way to break its influence over you."

"Probably. I just haven't found it yet."

"You will."

"I hope so. Okay, you ready for this?"

I wasn't, but we had no choice. We had to find a way to help those ghosts.

"As ready as I'll ever be," I said.

Kat released the clasps that held the book closed. They fell to the table with a gentle clink. I heard a soft laugh, the kind of laugh that maniacal killers in horror movies often spewed right before dispatching a victim. This one sounded like it was bubbling up from an underground cave.

Goosebumps scattered across my arms.

"Did you hear that?"

"What?" Kat said.

"The laugh."

"Um, no."

Maybe only someone like me could hear it.

"Must have been my imagination. I think I'm a little creeped out right now."

It wasn't my imagination, but I didn't tell Kat that. She was already uneasy enough having to look through the *Compendium*.

"Or maybe there is something to my theory after all," Kat said, frowning at the *Compendium*.

"Maybe. Don't witches have banishing spells for evil spirits or things like that?"

"We do. I tried one on this. Just in case, you know? It didn't work."

Kat peeled back the cover. On the first page, *Compendium Maleficium* was hand written in black ink in neat script. Kat turned page after page, eyes scanning the text, looking for some kind of spell to help the ghosts.

"Hey Kat, how old is this book?" I asked as she kept searching.

"Hundreds of years old. Why?"

"Just curious. What language is it written in? Latin?"

"Among others. Mostly Latin though."

"Can you read Latin?"

"A little."

"How do you know what you're reading?"

"I've read enough spells to know what a lot of the words in here mean. And what I don't know, I can infer. And I can pronounce them. That's the most important thing. Don't want to screw that up. That could be disastrous."

"Well, um, I guess that's practical." I didn't like this book any more than Kat did. I hoped she found something soon so she could stuff it back in the safety deposit box and we could leave.

"Here, I found something." She ran her finger under the words as she read silently to herself. "Bugger. This is complicated. I need to do this exactly right, or it's not going to work."

"What is it?"

"It's a working to undo a spirit summoning. It would let me reverse what Uriah has done."

"That's good, right?"

"Maybe." She chewed on her lip and flipped some more pages. "Here. This might work better. It's a banishing spell. It would send Ezekiel back to where he came from. I think this is what I need. It will be faster and more effective to send him straight back rather than try to undo someone else's work." She studied the page, her eyebrows scrunched together. "I just have to make sure I don't screw it up."

"You can memorize it, right?"

"I don't know. If I get one thing wrong, it *all* goes sideways." Her fingers drummed on the page as she worried her lower lip. "I'm going to have to take the *Compendium* with me. I'll have to read directly from it."

"What? Are you sure?"

"Believe me, I don't want to. I don't want this book to leave the bank, but I don't think I have a choice. I can't risk a mistake. We're only going to get one shot at this."

"Okay. I guess."

Kat closed the *Compendium*, then closed the lid on the safety deposit box. She tucked the *Compendium* under one arm and pushed the red button by the door.

After a minute the lady who had assisted us came in and took the safety deposit box.

"Is there anything else I can help you with today?" she asked.

"No, thank you," Kat said.

We followed her out, then diverged to the main part of the bank as she went back to the safety deposit vault. Kat clutched the book to her chest the entire walk back to my car. Bandit was in the back seat, staring out the window us.

We climbed in, Kat still with a death grip on the *Compendium*.

"You going to hold on to that book like that all day?" I asked as I pulled out of the parking space. There was a pinched look around Kat's eyes and mouth that had me worried.

"No," she said, casting a glance in my direction before turning her attention back to the traffic around us. "I'm going to put it in the storeroom once we get to Beltane. I don't like having it this close to me."

"That's probably a good idea. You going to be okay to use it up on Rainbow Hill?"

"Yes. I'll have to be. After that it goes right back in the box."

That sounded good to me. Seeing the effect it was having on Kat made me agree that the *Compendium* shouldn't be out in the world. Especially not in the hands of people like Uriah and Bruce. They weren't good people to begin with. I didn't even want to think how they would be influenced if it fell into their hands. It was too scary to think about.

Chapter 22

The day at the store was like any other. Kat was a little edgy and distracted for a while after we got there, but settled down after chatting with regular customers and busying herself restocking. I had nervous energy running through me all day. The anniversary of Ezekial's hanging was looming, which meant we were running out of time. We still had to figure out how we were going to get into the house on Rainbow Hill.

Five o'clock came sooner than I thought it would. I went to the door to flip the sign to 'closed' when Deedee suddenly appeared on the other side of it. Her shoulders were hunched, her arms wrapped around her midsection, eyebrows tilted in fear.

What was going on with Deedee?

I made a beckoning motion for her to come in. Everyone else had gone home, so only Kat and I were in the store.

She walked through the door, shoulders still drawn toward each other. After she was in a moment, she closed her eyes and let out a sigh. Her shoulders relaxed and she began to straighten.

She opened her eyes again as Bandit trotted over, eager to see his friend. Deedee reached down and scratched his ears, but didn't muster the usual enthusiasm she had for him.

"Deedee? Are you okay?" I asked. "What's the matter?"

Her eyes were still shadowed with worry.

"I'm not sure. I've been feeling funny since last night, and it's getting worse. It's much better in here though. I can't feel it anymore."

"Feel what?"

"This pulling sensation. I mean, I noticed it a little before, when I told you about the spirits, but it was like background noise. I just kind of ignored it. But now it's a lot stronger, and a lot harder to ignore. I think if it got any stronger, I wouldn't be able to ignore it anymore. I would have to follow it."

"That's what the new ghosts have been feeling," I said as Kat wandered over.

"What's going on?" she asked.

"Deedee's here. She's feeling the same pull as the ghosts in the basement."

"Oh wow. I didn't know older ghosts could feel that."

"Some can. Chester could, a little, but not Elsbeth."

"What ghosts in what basement?" asked Deedee, her eyes darting between me and Kat.

"Those ghosts you told me about, that Elsbeth saw, were being drawn to a basement in a house up on Rainbow Hill. They're up there now." I didn't mention that some had been pulled into some other dimension.

"Oh my gosh! That's terrible. Why are they going there?"

"Someone is making them. He has a beacon that's drawing them. That's what you're feeling."

Deedee shuddered.

"I don't like the feeling. How can I make it go away?"

"You can't, but maybe Kat and I can. We're going to try."

"I don't know what to do until then," Deedee said, rubbing her arms. "If I go back out there, I'm going to feel it again. Then I might end up in that basement too."

"Why don't you stay here for now? Is that okay with you, Kat, if Deedee stays here until we stop Uriah and Bruce? The wards around the store keep her from feeling that pulling sensation."

Kat was only getting half the conversation, but she nodded.

"If she's safer here, of course she can stay."

"Tell her I said thanks," Deedee said, giving Kat a warm smile only I could see.

"She says, 'Thanks'," I told Kat.

"Oh, okay," Kat said, her eyes looking studiously at the space in front of me as if she thought she might see Deedee if she stared hard enough. "You're welcome."

"Thank you too, Cami," Deedee said.

"What for?"

"For always being a good friend, and for trying to help me, and the others, now. Most people aren't as nice as you. I don't think many would try to help ghosts, even if they could see us. You're always kind to all of us. It's one of the reasons we're drawn to you."

"You're drawn to me?"

"Sure, in a way. Your kindness, and this warm energy about you makes spirits want to be near you. That's why so many of us talk to you. I don't know what kind of beacon this person who is drawing these spirits has, but you're like a beacon to us too. Only a good one."

I blinked away tears as Deedee's words sank in.

"I didn't know that."

I'd never had any idea that the spirits I had encountered since I was a child saw me that way. I always thought they spoke to me out of loneliness, or a desire to connect to the living.

"You're special, Cami. Not just because you can see us, but because of who you are."

"Thanks, Deedee."

I knelt down in front of Bandit. His beautiful eyes fixed on me, head tilting to the left.

"I want you to stay here with Deedee, buddy."

"Rooooooooo."

Bandit backed up, head lowering. He wanted to go with me.

"She needs you right now. I don't want her to be here alone. She's our friend, and we have to look out for her."

Bandit whined, ears back. He came over to me and put his nose inches from mine. Tears prickled the back of my eyes.

"I know you want to go with me, but I need you to be here, okay? Look after Deedee."

Deedee having company wasn't my only reason for leaving Bandit behind. I didn't want him anywhere near that basement. I had no idea what was going to happen down there, but the last thing I wanted was for my dog to be in the middle of it. The thought of him being in any kind of danger was more than I could handle right now.

"Thank you, Cami," Deedee said. She knelt on one knee and put an arm around Bandit. "We'll be okay here, right boy?"

He gave her cheek a quick lick, then focused anxious eyes back on me.

"We'll be back as soon as we can," I said.

We left them in the safety of Beltane Books, Deedee waving goodbye to us as Bandit sat by her feet, his eyes tracking me until we rounded the corner. My heart ached leaving him behind.

"Let's head back to my house," I said as we climbed in my car. I missed Bandit already, but I knew leaving him was the right decision.

"Okay. I'm going to study the *Compendium* a little more to see if there's anything else I can use," she said, absentmindedly patting the book on her lap. "Are there any ghosts you want to check on before we get there?"

"No, I don't think so. Elsbeth is far older than Chester, and most of the others I know are older than Deedee, so they should be—"

Nausea rolled over me as a realization hit me.

"Cami? What's wrong? You're white as a sheet."

"There's one ghost who's younger than all of them," I said, bile crawling up my throat. "Wynn's mom. If Deedee is barely able to ignore the stronger pull, there's no way Helen could."

"Oh, *crap*," Kat said. "I forgot about her. That does it. We're going in tomorrow morning. We're out of time anyway."

"But how? We need the house to be empty."

"I think I can take care of that."

Kat pulled her phone out of her purse, tapped the screen a few times, then put it to her ear.

"Hello, Bruce? Hi, it's Kat. Listen, I was wondering if you could meet me at my house tomorrow morning before the store opens." She paused and I could hear a man's muted voice. "I want to talk to you about Greg's funeral. I could use some help, and since you're good at organizing things, and Greg's friend, I thought you might want to be involved." I heard Bruce's voice again. "You will? Thanks, I really appreciate it. Eight o'clock alright? Oh, good. I'll see you tomorrow morning."

Kat hung up, her expression grim.

"With any luck both he and Uriah will show up," she said. "Meanwhile, we'll be at that house getting those ghosts out of there."

"Kat, you're brilliant."

She smiled.

"Well, you know."

Chapter 23

My nerves were jittering in overdrive when we pulled up to my house. I still had no idea what I was going to do once we got into that basement. It was all going to hinge on Kat, and whether or not she could disrupt the hold that beacon had on the spirits, and nullify that summoning circle.

My phone buzzed right after I killed the engine. It was Wynn texting me. He had twelve-hour night shifts at the ER for the rest of the week, so texting or phone calls were our only option since we couldn't get together. He was saying hi and wondering how my day was going. I had no clue what to tell him. The last twenty-four hours had been bizarre. To say the least.

"That Wynn?" Kat asked as we got out of the car, her smile lighting up her eyes.

"Yep. He's at the hospital and wants to know what I've been up to."

Kat's eyes widened. "Not sure how you should answer that question."

"What? You don't want me to tell him that your house got broken into by the two guys who killed your friend, we retrieved an evil book from the bank, and we're planning to use it tomorrow morning to free a bunch of trapped ghosts? Whatever would be wrong with that?"

Kat laughed.

"Go for it. He's an open-minded guy. I'm sure he could handle it."

"Yeah, maybe not," I said, chuckling. "I think I'll leave things like ghosts and magic books as topics of discussion for when we've been dating a little longer. Like twenty years."

Kat grinned as we reached the door.

"Probably a good idea. I mean, maybe not twenty years, but perhaps not just yet."

I dug my keys out of my purse and unlocked the front door.

"What sounds good for dinner?" I asked as we entered the house.

"Anything you...Wizard?"

Kat's familiar was lying in a grey heap on the floor near the entrance to the kitchen. She rushed over to her cat just as Uriah stepped into the doorway behind Wizard.

"KAT!"

An arm like steel wrapped itself around my neck from behind, squeezing hard enough to keep me still, but not to choke off my air. A firm chest pressed against my back as a black gloved hand holding a folded white cloth flew at me from the right and slapped over the lower half of my face. My nostrils filled with a sweet, pungent smell as Uriah swung a right hook at Kat. She dropped to the floor next to her beloved familiar.

I clawed at the hand over my face, trying to pry it off. I might as well have been trying to open a bear trap. I tried to twist in my captor's grip, loosen his arm, but it was futile. He was too strong. The edges of my vision began to close in as my assailant pressed the cloth more firmly to my face.

Uriah stepped over Kat, shaking his right hand and flexing his fingers. His black eyes fixed on me, a cruel smile twisting his lips.

"Night, night," he said as the arm tightened on my neck and I succumbed to darkness.

Chapter 24

C hapter 24

A new, musty smell besieged my nose. I struggled to open my eyes. It was like trying to lift weights at the gym with noodle arms. Finally, after three attempts, they struggled open. There was nothing but pale grey in front of me. I blinked, my brain still fuzzy. Why couldn't I see anything but grey?

After my eyes focused, I realized I was staring at a wall. I heard muffled sounds behind me, and a man's voice. My ears weren't working right yet either. My head felt like it was stuffed with cotton. So did my mouth. Probably because there was a rag shoved in it. It was coarse and tasted like moth balls smelled.

Where was I?

I tried to roll on my back, but my body didn't want to cooperate yet. My stomach lurched as nausea and dizziness washed over me. The wall in front of me distorted in weird waves, and my head swam. After a moment or two it was just a wall again. My stomach gave another twinge, then settled down.

I debated another attempt at trying to roll over. Something was wrapped around my wrists so tightly they hurt. My bleary gaze drifted down my body. White zip ties encircled my wrists, and my ankles. The flesh around my wrists was bulging like sausage trying to escape the casing. My fingers tingled from lack of circulation. I tried flexing my hands; it was like they were made of clay.

The voice behind me spoke again, saying words I didn't understand.

Uriah.

It was Uriah.

I forced my body to move and flopped onto my back. My heart hammered and my wrists throbbed. Beads of sweat sprouted on my forehead. Dim light barely illuminated the cobweb covered ceiling that hung above me. Stiffness in my neck from being squeezed make it hard to look to my left.

My stomach rolled again. I was in the basement on Rainbow Hill.

Uriah, clad in his black cloak, was on his knees in front of the summoning circle. On the ground next to him on the right was the *Compendium Maleficium*, open to a page about a third the way through the book. More ghosts than ever were crammed into the basement, some only within feet of the circle because there were so many of them. The ghosts I had seen before were still huddled near the wall. Greg was closer to the circle, his arms around a female ghost I didn't recognize. Her fingers gripped his Hawaiian shirt with tight fists, eyes wide and terrified.

Wynn's mom, Helen, was only a few feet away from him. She was watching Uriah, wrapped in her own arms, her expression pensive. She was one of the few ghosts in the basement that wasn't crying. My movement caught her attention; her expression changed to shock when she saw it was me. She opened her mouth to say something, but

I shook my head. I didn't want to take any chance that Uriah would hear her. He had been able to hear Bandit the night we had spied on him. I didn't want to risk his attention being drawn to me in any way right now.

Helen nodded at me, then fixed her eyes back on Uriah, and what was around him.

On the ground about six feet to Uriah's left, near the spirit beacon, lay Kat. Her eyes were closed. There was a nasty, purplish bruise sprouting on the left side of her face where Uriah had slugged her. Her hands and feet were secured together with zip ties too. Behind her stood Bruce, his gaze fixed on Uriah. He wore the same cowled cloak as Uriah, and the expression of someone who was about to get everything they ever wanted. He and Uriah were getting ready to bring Ezekiel over. I had to stop them, but I had no clue how.

I rolled over on to my side so I could see them better, and look around me. About six feet from my head, against the adjacent wall, was a light grey, plastic storage rack with boxes on the top shelf, and plastic buckets and garden fertilizer on the middle rack. On the bottom shelf I could see pruning shears, hand trowels and rakes, and foam kneeling pads. Leaning against the rack in the corner was a shovel with a long wooden handle. Why did Bruce have all this stuff since there was nothing planted around the house except a few trees? Maybe he was planning on moving in after he brought Ezekiel over.

My hands began to throb steadily. I was losing more circulation. I had to get the zip ties off me. First, I needed to get closer to that rack. I tried to push myself up on my elbow when suddenly Bruce's head swiveled toward me.

Crap.

He walked over to me and knelt down on one knee, his grey eyes like chips of flint.

"I see you're awake," he said in a low voice. "Just in time to participate in our ritual."

"Mmmmmmmmmm."

"What? Oh. Just a moment." He pulled the rag out of my mouth. "What was that, Cami? And please, keep your voice down. We don't want to disturb Uriah."

"Why are you two doing this? What on earth do you hope to gain by bringing over the spirit of Ezekiel Blackmore?"

"Been doing a little digging I see. Let's just say that Santa Theresa screwed over my family, and it's time to right old wrongs."

"You mean that they took your family's land away? You're still angry about that?"

"That land was *ours*," Bruce replied through clenched teeth. "We bought it, we worked it, it was ours. But they took it from us because we stood up for ourselves. And because we were different. When the fine citizens found out my family followed a different spiritual path other than the one that takes you to church every Sunday, they used it as an excuse to strip my family of the land we owned and lived on for generations."

"No one in Santa Theresa today had anything to do with that. You can't hold them accountable for something that happened generations ago."

"Can't I? Do you think anything has really changed? Do you think half the people in this town would be so nice to people like Kat and Greg if they knew they were witches? How long do you think before her store had a brick thrown through the window? Or business dried up? Not long, I think."

"You're wrong," I said. "This isn't the 1800's. People are much more open minded these days. Plenty of people know Kat is a witch and they have no problem with it."

"Am I? I don't think as many people as you think know about the coven, or who belongs to it. There's no sign hanging outside the covenstead like there is outside a church, or synagogue, or mosque. They keep things quiet, and for good reason."

"Just because they don't advertise doesn't mean they're being secretive because they're worried about what people will do to them. People here aren't like that."

"You give them too much credit. It wasn't that long ago that witches were still being run out of this narrow minded, hick town. There was a minor witch hunt here in the 1930's. Bet you didn't know about that. Back then even Kat's beautiful red hair would have made her a suspect. The descendants of those people still live here. I doubt they're any more open minded than their ancestors."

"That doesn't mean you should unleash an evil spirit on the town. What are you going to do with him once you do? Do you actually think you can control him?"

"With the spells in the *Compendium* I know I can. Thank you for delivering that to us, by the way. Ezekiel will be at my beck and call. With him I'm going to do what my ancestors should have done, if only they'd known how, and known that they had a spirit like Ezekiel to work with. If they'd only had a book like the *Compendium*."

I broke out in a clammy sweat at the mere thought of what they might try to do with the malevolent spirit they were trying to bring over.

"Why are Kat and I here? What do you want with us?" I wasn't sure I wanted an answer to that question, but I had to ask anyway.

He glanced over his shoulder at Uriah whose voice was rising, his chanting becoming more intense.

"I guess there's no harm in telling you. You and Kat are going to help fuel the ritual. The spirit of a witch is a powerful thing, much more powerful than a normal spirit, which is why we killed not only Greg, but Evelyn, another coven member, as well. She met her end before our visit to your house." Was that the spirit that was clinging to Greg? "Oh yes, and we killed Leonard and Merriam too, right after we killed Evelyn. They were shacking up together, so we got a two for one."

I glanced over at the ghosts around Greg. There were so many new faces in the basement. Any of them could have been the murdered witches. Greg was still holding the same woman, making small circles on her back with his hand as she sobbed into his shirt.

"Anyway," Bruce continued, "at the peak of the ritual I am going to cut Kat's throat. The release of her spirit will complete the level of power we need to bring over Ezekiel's spirit."

"Right after you sacrifice those poor, innocent spirits."

"*Yes*," he said, looking at me intently. "Spirits you can *see*. I was very surprised when Uriah told me you're a medium. He suspected when he caught you spying on him. I thought he might be right that night at dinner. You have a different feel about you than other people do."

"A feel?"

"Almost like an aura. Your connection to the dead emanates something akin to power."

"And you know what that feels like?"

"I do. I can't see ghosts, but I can sense things about people, at least if I spend some time around them."

He reached out his right hand and caressed my cheek with his index finger. He laughed when I jerked my face away.

"You, my dear, as a medium, are the icing on the cake. The cherry on the ice cream sundae." My heart shuddered. "You're going to be the final sacrifice. The ghost, the essence, of a medium, is even more powerful. Your spirit will feed Ezekiel once he crosses over. It won't make him corporeal, but it will give him the power to affect the plane. Once he devours your spirit he will be able to do everything I want him to. And what he wants to do. He has some scores to settle too. Santa Theresa will never be the same again."

My mouth was suddenly devoid of all moisture as I imagined the havoc he, Uriah, and Ezekiel would wreak.

"Please," I whispered. "Don't do this. Those ghosts don't deserve to be sent to whatever hell, or dark spirit realm, Ezekiel is in. They've done nothing wrong. And Kat's never done anything to you. She and the coven welcomed you."

"The ghosts are a necessary sacrifice. Besides, you should be more worried about yourself. As to Kat, she never liked me. In fact, she hoped to find a way to get me ousted. She probably would have, especially after she did some digging. Don't think I fell for that ruse about a display in the store. I knew you two were up to something else entirely."

"That's why you killed Greg. So he couldn't help us."

"Yes, and I wanted his spirit. I needed to slow you two down. Couldn't risk being outed before tonight, the eve of the anniversary of Ezekiel's hanging."

He pushed the rag toward my face.

"Wait—"

The taste of the rag made my stomach lurch as he crammed it in my mouth.

"Sorry, Cami. Not that I haven't enjoyed our little chat, but midnight is approaching. The 13th. The ritual will soon be complete, and I need to play my part."

He went over to Kat, knelt next to her, and slapped her bruised face. Her eyelids fluttered as she struggled to regain consciousness.

"Come on, Kat. I need you awake. And afraid. Your spirit will much more potent if you die terrified."

He slapped her again. This time her eyes fluttered open. She recoiled when she saw Bruce looming over her. He reached inside his cloak and pulled out a seven-inch-long serrated knife.

Kat's eyes bugged in her head.

"There we go," he said, his mouth parting in a nasty grin. "That's the fear I'm looking for."

He grabbed a fistful of Kat's hair and hauled her to her knees, facing the circle. I could hear her muffled, pained protests. He stepped behind her, standing to the left of Uriah, his gaze fixed on the circle while Uriah continued to chant. It might have been in Latin, but I wasn't sure. Uriah's eyes were fixed on the book as he read, his body rocking back and forth slightly as he spoke.

A few of the ghosts were crying hysterically while they watched Bruce manhandle Kat and listened to the ritual being performed. Others were shaking, their faces frozen in grimaces of horror. Their fate was going to be sealed once the ritual was complete, and there wasn't a thing they could do about it. I had to stop this somehow.

I looked around me again. I couldn't just lie here while Bruce murdered my friend. My eyes fixed on some garden clippers. They were going to be my best bet for cutting the zip ties.

I rolled onto my belly and used my elbows and forearms to pull me along the floor while pushing with my feet. As I crawled quietly forward like a drunken caterpillar, I kept Bruce and Uriah in my peripheral vision. The last thing I needed was for either of them to notice what I was doing. Luckily for me Bruce began echoing what Uriah was chanting, repeating everything he said, completely engrossed in the ritual. He was paying no attention to me. The jerk probably thought there was nothing I could do anyway.

I was hoping to prove him wrong.

After almost a minute of scooching I got over to the rack. I reached for a pair of clippers with a red handle and fumbled with the blade release. My fingers felt like half-numb, overstuffed sausages from the lack of circulation. The throbbing didn't help either. I could barely feel the clippers in my hand. I pushed my thumb against the release, but it didn't want to give.

C'mon, you stupid clippers!

I pushed harder, wedging my thumb against the release. The clippers popped out of my hands and made a soft thud when they hit the ground. I froze, waiting for Uriah or Bruce to hear. Neither turned. They hadn't noticed over their chanting. I breathed a sigh of relief and grabbed the clippers again. This time when I pushed the blade release it gave and the clippers popped open. *Finally*.

Now I had to figure out a way to use them. I needed to wedge the clippers in place somehow and steady them. I pushed off a bit from the ground with my forearms and brought my knees under me. Then I pushed myself up with my hands, picked up the clippers, nearly dropped them again as my hands fumbled to hold them, and put the handles between my knees so that the blades were facing up.

Uriah's voice became louder, more intense. He reached for the same silver bowl he had used when I spied on him. His fingertips circled the edge of the bowl while he chanted. I had to hurry. There wasn't much more time before he called the spirits into the summoning circle.

I slid my wrists slowly over the lower blade, trying to gingerly slip the sharp edge between my wedged together wrists. I was almost there when the sharp edge nicked my flesh as it pushed against me, a small pinch of pain that yielded a shallow cut. Finally, I got the edge positioned against the zip tie.

I rubbed the plastic of the zip tie against the lower blade of the clippers, up, down, up, down, up, down, when, *snap*! The plastic gave and the zip tie fell into my lap. I bit back a moan as a stinging avalanche of blood rushed into my hands. I shook them in an effort to get the blood moving normally again. Then I took the rag out of my mouth and threw it on the floor. My mouth was so dry it was as if I had sucked on old sweat socks. I shook my hands again as some of the feeling returned. I couldn't sit here much longer. Uriah was almost ready to move on to the next phase of the ritual.

I took the clippers again, then shifted onto my hip and swung my legs around. I gripped the them as tightly as I could and cut the zip ties around my ankles. A brief flash of relief washed over me. My arms and legs were free.

I put the clippers on the ground and pushed myself up to a wobbly stand. My head swam again, probably still aftereffects of whatever they knocked me out with. I took a deep breath and quietly wrapped my hands around the handle of the shovel that was leaning against the wall. I lifted it to my right shoulder, steadying it as I crept up behind Bruce and Uriah.

I had a split second to decide which of them I needed to take out first. I twisted my body, brought the shovel back behind me in a fast, fluid arc, and *swung*.

Chapter 25

The shovel connected with Uriah's skull with a loud *thunk*. He fell forward and did a faceplant in the middle of the summoning circle. The silver bowl rolled out of his hand, its liquid contents splashing all over the ground. I didn't have time to register what it was because Bruce tossed Kat aside and lunged for me so fast, I barely stepped out of his reach in time.

A red flush of rage covered his face from hairline to neckline.

"You bitch!" He lunged at me again, flicking his blade at me in a blur. It came within inches of my arm as I sidestepped it and raised the shovel again. "I am *not* going to let you stop this ritual. I've waited too long for this!"

"Up yours, Bruce. If you think I'm just going to lie there and let you murder me and my friend, then you've got a screw loose. Judging from what you're doing down here, you clearly do."

I swung the shovel at Bruce, but it didn't have as much momentum as when I rung Uriah's bell. He ducked under it, slashing at me again.

This time he missed me by a hair. I shuffled backwards, my feet still wobbly from being tied up.

"You need to die at the right moment, but that doesn't mean I can't cut you up a little before then. Throw down that shovel and I promise I'll make your death quick. If you don't, I'm going to carve pieces out of you before you die."

"You can try," I said, circling to my left a little so that I could see Kat out of the corner of my eye. She was still lying on the ground, struggling to get on her hands and knees despite tied hands and feet. She almost made it when she lost her balance and flopped back onto the ground. Uriah was on the ground too, groaning, and rubbing his head.

I couldn't worry about either one right now. I had to deal with Bruce.

This time, instead of swinging at Bruce with the shovel, I jabbed at him with the point. He reared back, tilting his head and upper body left and right while I stabbed the shovel at him, trying to drive him backwards toward the wall opposite the rack with gardening equipment.

The ghosts had stopped crying and were watching me and Bruce with baited breath. I still had to figure out how I was going to stop this maniac and help not only me and Kat, but them. I brought the shovel to my shoulder again to make Bruce think I was going to swing at him. As he lunged forward to make use of an opportunity to slash at me with his knife, I stepped forward on my left foot, cocked my right leg like the hammer on a pistol, and kicked him with everything I had right in the gonads.

"Aaarrgh!"

He collapsed onto his knees, forehead on the floor, butt in the air.

I made a mad, wobbly dash for the clippers, snatched them off the floor, and stumbled over to Kat. I dropped the shovel next to her and scrambled onto my knees. I pulled the rag out of her mouth and chucked it over my shoulder.

"Hold still," I said, gently maneuvering the clippers under the zip tie so I could cut her wrists free.

I heard a quick *snick* at the same time I heard Greg yell out, "Cami, behind you!"

His warning came a fraction too late. I turned just in time to get clobbered in the face with the *Compendium*. Pain exploded around my nose. I fell back, my head thumping onto the hard floor, my eyes watering from the pain that was spreading from my nose across my cheeks. The clippers skittered out of my hand as I hit the ground. Through my blurry vision I saw Uriah kick Kat viciously in the ribs, then turn back to me.

He threw the book on the ground, put his feet on either side of me, dropped onto my chest, put his hands on my throat, and squeezed. My hands flew to his, trying to pry them off my windpipe. Not only did his fingers not give even a little, they continued to tighten. I swiped at his face, trying to scratch him, reach his eyes to dig at those, anything, but he reared back, avoided all my attempts. My chest grew tight, not just from his weight sitting on it, but from lack of oxygen. My face throbbed even more as the blood pounded in my veins. Spots danced around the edge of my vision, and just as things started to go grey, I heard a *thwak*.

Uriah's hands let go as he slid off me and dropped onto the floor. Kat stood behind him holding the shovel, swaying, panting, face flushed. She had managed to untie her feet in time to save me.

I took a huge breath into my lungs, trying to get my vision to clear and my brain to function again. Then I rolled on my side and pushed myself to my knees. Bruce was righting himself too and reaching for his knife. I scrambled to my feet, stumbling as the room see-sawed. Kat leaned on the shovel, panting, her face pale.

Uriah groaned and rolled onto his back.

"Get up!" Bruce barked at him, his left hand over his injured junk. He was having a hard time straightening up. "Take care of that damn witch, then finish the frigging ritual."

Uriah mumbled something incoherent as he pushed himself off the ground. He gave me a furious look and rubbed his head.

"I'll get it done," he said, glaring at Bruce. "Just keep that bitch from bashing me in the head again."

Bruce rounded on me, face red with rage. I tried to shuffle backward, but the room was still tilting and my feet didn't want to work properly. In an instant he flicked the knife out so fast I couldn't even back up to get out of range. Instinctively I threw my left arm up to protect myself. Pain flared down my arm as the blade sliced a deep, four-inch-long incision down the outside of my forearm. He had cut right along the bone. I saw a flash of off-white when I clutched my arm to my chest and staggered backward.

Behind him I saw Uriah and Kat struggling, each with their hands on the handle of the long shovel. Kat was desperately trying to hold on while Uriah attempted to wrench the tool out of her hands. The ghosts were crying again, but I couldn't do anything at that moment except wonder how I was going to keep Bruce from killing me.

He feinted at me again. I dodged, barely keeping out of reach of the knife. My arm was throbbing worse than my face, and a steady river of blood ran down to my elbow and dripped onto the floor. Uriah wrested the shovel violently out of Kat's hands. She lost her balance and fell backward, careening into the only metal storage rack in the basement. Her head bounced hard off the edge, then whiplashed to the side. She dropped to the ground in a heap just as Bruce took another swipe at me.

I avoided him again, but I knew I wasn't going to be able to dodge him much longer. I was almost to the wall under the window, where I had woken up. A couple more steps and I would be out of room. I had to do something, *now*.

Uriah was back at the circle, chanting again. In front of him, in the middle of the summoning circle, the rift began to open, purple light creeping out of the tear. It would only be another minute or two before he sacrificed the ghosts.

They screamed when Ezekiel's face began to push itself into view.

I was out of time. My only chance was to get Bruce off balance. Just as he started to slash the knife at me again, I rushed him, my hands thrust out in front of me in an attempt to catch the arm holding the knife. My left hand closed on his wrist, my right on the hand with the knife. My body slammed into his, the knife trapped between us. He staggered backward, eyes wide with surprise, my momentum carrying us to the ground.

"Gurck."

Bruce's mouth was open, breath wheezing out of it. I rolled off him and pushed myself to my knees. The knife was embedded in Bruce's gut to the hilt right under his ribcage. I clutched my bleeding arm to my chest as purple light began to fill the basement. Uriah was in the final stage.

The ghosts were screaming, trying to get as far away from the summoning circle as they could. I had to stop Uriah. I glanced at Bruce, at the knife in his chest. He was still alive, but not by much. If he died, his spirit would help fuel the circle. If I didn't stop Uriah, he was going to finish the ritual and the ghosts would be pulled into the hell dimension.

I had no choice.

I grabbed the handle of the knife, and pulled. Another wheeze passed Bruce's lips and his eyes fluttered shut.

I put the knife in my left hand and slowly pushed myself to my feet with my right. Uriah was reading from the *Compendium*, his voice intense, rhythmic. His hand shot out, pointing at the ghosts, his voice rising to the point he was almost yelling. The ghosts began to move forward, sliding toward the circle. Their screams rang in my ears as Ezekiel's face fully formed in the shimmer of the rift. Some of the ghosts entered the circle and the tear grew.

"Do it now!" Ezekiel snarled. "Finish the ritual!"

I staggered toward the circle, trying to keep my knees from buckling. Blood loss was making me woozy. The front of my shirt was soaked in blood from clutching my arm to my chest, but I didn't have time to stop the bleeding. Uriah's form was fuzzier around the edges than it had been a few minutes ago.

Uriah's voice rose as the first of the ghosts were sucked toward the portal. The spirits behind them tried to hold on to them, to drag them back, but it was useless. Ezekiel's face split in an evil grin, anticipation of crossing over flooding his eyes. The man from the hospital was the closest to the rift and now fully engulfed in purple light, sobbing as Ezekiel loomed over him.

The portal grew, elongating and widening. Ezekiel's entire head and most of his neck was now visible. I was frozen in place, staring at the hideous face of Ezekiel Blackmore while more ghosts slid into the summoning circle, their bodies pressed up against the man from the hospital, who now whimpered in terror.

The purple glow pulsed as Bruce's ghost suddenly appeared in my peripheral vision at the edge of the circle. His eyes were wide while he looked around as if he was still trying to adjust to his transition. He took a few halting steps toward Ezekiel, his gaze now riveted on the spirit he had been longing to bring over.

"You're almost here, Master," he said in an entranced voice.

"Yes, and you're just what I need," said the looming spirit.

Ezekiel snatched at Bruce's cloak and hauled him through the rift. I could hear the echo of his scream as he disappeared into the void. The rift pulsed again, growing wide enough that Ezekiel was able to push an enormous arm and a tree trunk sized leg through the rift and reach for the nearest ghost. His hand clamped onto the collar of the man from the hospital and jerked him toward the portal.

I took another lurching step forward when something bright rushed by me.

"ROOOOOOOOOOOO!!!"

NO! Bandit!

My dog was in the basement, rocketing right for Ezekiel, and he was glowing. A soft, white light I had never seen before surrounded him like a halo. It pushed back the sickly purple glow where he stood, illuminating the ground around him. Every hackle on the back of his neck and along his spine was raised, and his head was lowered. A menacing snarl rumbled out of his chest through bared teeth.

"Rowwwrrrrr!"

He lunged for Ezekiel, snapping at the leg that was clear of the rift. The glow around him continued to push through the purple light. Ezekiel had to squint his eyes in order to look down at his attacker.

Ezekiel let go of the hospital man and lunged for Bandit. Bandit leapt back, snapping at the hand, trying to drive Ezekiel back. The murderer swiped at him, but Bandit barked and snarled, putting himself between Ezekiel and the terrified ghosts, all the while dodging Ezekiel's attempts to grab him.

I tried to move forward again, my knees buckling as I shuffled my feet. I had to get to the summoning circle and stop this monster somehow. Our lives, and my dog, depended on it. I took a deep breath and willed the room to steady as Bandit snapped and snarled, trying to drive Ezekiel back into his own dimension.

With a rage filled grunt Ezekiel pushed further through the rift and lunged for my dog. This time his reach was enough. His huge hand sank into Bandit's fur and twisted. Bandit yelped as Ezekiel's fingers dug viciously into his hide. Then Ezekiel started to pull my dog into the rift.

Oh my god.

"BANDIT!"

Adrenaline and fear for my beloved boy got my swaying body moving. I transferred the knife into my right hand, staggered forward, and plunged it into Uriah's back. He screamed, the hand that had been pointing at the ghosts now desperately reaching back over his shoulder. His hand flexed open and shut, then he fell forward. He hit the ground, mouth open like a carp, eyes glazed with shock.

"NOOOOOOOOOOOOOOOO!!!!!"

Ezekiel's roar thundered in my ears.

Bandit was twisting in his grasp but couldn't get free. I couldn't help him because I couldn't touch my dog! Panic seized my lungs like a vice, choking off my air. *No, no, no, no!*

I looked around wildly for anything that might help when Helen ran past the other ghosts and threw herself on Bandit, wrapping her arms around him and tearing him out of Ezekiel's hand. The glow enveloped both of them, and suddenly Helen looked more like a celestial warrior than the mother of my boyfriend.

"You leave that dog alone, you monster," she said, her eyes flashing with fury. "You leave all of us alone!"

Ezekiel swiped at Helen, clipping her on the head as she tried to duck. She staggered to one knee, but recovered and got back on her feet just out of reach of Ezekiel's flailing grasp.

"Stick it where the sun doesn't shine, mister. You're *not* getting this dog."

She held on to a wriggling Bandit for all she was worth and retreated out of the circle.

"I will snap your neck like a twig, you foolish woman!"

"Let's see you try," she said, glaring at Ezekiel. "Hold still, puppy," she said in a more soothing tone. "I'm not going to let him get you."

Ezekiel pushed more of himself through the portal. Even though Uriah was facedown and no longer chanting, the ritual somehow continued to be active. Bandit was still struggling and barking, but Helen clung to him. She knew he was doomed if Ezekiel got ahold of him again.

To Ezekiel's left, Kat, pale and battered, staggered to her feet, blood running down the side of her face. She stumbled over to the circle, then dropped to her knees next to the *Compendium Maleficium*.

"Hurry, Kat," I said, doing everything I could to stay standing. My legs were like jelly. I was lightheaded from the blood loss, and my arm hurt badly. "The rift is open. Ezekiel is halfway over."

"Give me a second," she said in a breathless voice as she grabbed the *Compendium*.

"How dare you! Unhand that book!" Ezekiel yelled.

The spirits that had been dragged almost to the rift began to fight their way to the edge of the circle. Ezekiel ignored them, his murderous eyes focused solely on Kat. He grunted while he pushed even farther into our plane, now only one leg left anchored in the portal.

Kat leafed through the book, flipping through the pages as fast as she could. She was looking for the banishing spell she saw when we were at the bank. She found the page she wanted and began to read, the words coming out of her mouth seeming to drip with power. I got goosebumps on my arms as she spoke. The feeling of magic was coming off her in waves.

The purple light began to fade, the tear closing, pushing Ezekiel back.

"STOP!" Ezekiel bellowed.

Kat's voice rose, the words pouring out of her faster, with more determination. Ezekiel was pulled backward, the portal closing around him as he struggled. As she spoke the final words the rift snapped shut, the purple light disappearing as if someone had flipped a switch.

"Go to hell, you bastard," she said, breathing heavy. "Go straight to hell."

Chapter 26

I almost cried with relief as I dropped to my knees next to Kat.

  She put her arms around me and hugged me like our lives depended on it.

I looked at Uriah, thinking he might still be alive, but he was utterly still. I could feel his spirit still lingering in his body. Not all emerged immediately. I didn't want to see his ghost. Seeing his body was enough.

I glanced past the circle. The ghosts were crying, but this time with happiness, not fear.

We had one thing left to do. The spirit beacon needed to be destroyed. Until it was, the ghosts couldn't leave the basement.

"Is there anything in the book that will take care of that candle?" I asked Kat after she released me.

"If I can put out the flame," she said, "that should do the trick."

She closed her eyes and reached a hand toward the candle.

"*Ignes extingue*," she said. The flame stuttered, but didn't go out.

"*Ignes extingue! Ignes extingue!*" The flamed stuttered again, almost as if it was fighting her spell, but stubbornly wouldn't go out.

"Damn it," Kat muttered. "So much for a simple spell. Guess it was too much to hope for."

She began leafing through the *Compendium* again, searching. After a moment she stopped, her index finger seeking something out on the page.

She took in a deep breath and said with as much force as she could muster, "*Expelle spiritus ignus! Abito! Abito!*" The flame guttered again, but struggled to hang on. "*Expelle spiritus ignus! Abito!*" Kat yelled, swaying as she fought to put out the spirit beacon.

The flame flicked and writhed, then after a last gasp, guttered out. My shoulders sagged.

It was out. It was finally *out*.

I turned to the ghosts, who were wide eyed and bewildered.

"You're free. You can go. You can pass over now."

At first, none of them moved. Then they came forward, crowded around us, their eyes fixed on us.

"Thank you," Greg said. "Thank you both for saving us from that." The other ghosts began murmuring, wiping tears away. His eyes watered too when he looked down at his friend. "Tell Kat I love her, that she's a wonderful friend, and that I'll miss her."

"I will," I promised.

The rest of the ghosts thanked us too, then began drifting away. Some of them started to glow, their interrupted transition to the next realm beginning again. Others drifted through the walls, maybe to return to their point of origin before they passed over. The only one that remained was Helen. She put Bandit, who had stopped glowing and wriggling when Ezekiel disappeared, down. He trotted over to me, his eyes anxiously fixed on my bleeding arm.

"Thank you," she said. "I don't know what was waiting for us over there, but you both saved us from it. For that I'm extremely grateful."

"Thank you for saving my dog," I said. My throat got tight as I looked at my border collie. "I don't know what I would have done if Ezekiel had condemned him to that hell dimension."

"He's a good boy," she said, smiling down at Bandit. She eyed my arm. "You need to wrap something around that. You're losing too much blood."

I looked down at my arm. It was still clutched it to my chest. My shirt was soaked all the way down to my jeans.

I looked back up to reply, but as I did Helen winked out of the basement. It was just as well. I didn't have much left in me for a long conversation.

"Bandit, go back to Deedee, okay?"

"Roooooooo." His nose was by my arm. He was worried and wanted to stay with me.

"We're all done here, buddy. We're leaving. Go back to Deedee. She's probably worried sick about you. Go back so that she knows everything's okay."

"Rooo."

Bandit stared at me for another moment, then ran toward the stairs and dissipated.

I breathed a sigh of relief, then glanced behind me at Bruce. My stomach churned. I killed him. I stared at Uriah. I killed him too. I just *killed* two men.

I crawled a few feet away from Kat and threw up. I wiped a shaking hand across my mouth while my stomach tried to wrench again.

The warm touch of Kat's hand settled on my back. I forced back tears as I turned to my friend.

"I can't believe I just killed two people."

"You saved our lives," she said, her voice strained. She was as beaten up as I was. "It's not like they left you a choice."

"I know, it's just..."

She nodded, unshed tears glistening in her lovely green eyes.

"We need to wrap that," Kat said, blinking at my arm.

"Yeah," I said. My head was swimmy again. The ground kept trying to reach for my face.

Kat's head swiveled around, looking for something to use. There was a lot of junk around the perimeter of the basement, but nothing made of cloth except for some dirty rags. She grabbed the bottom of her shirt and ripped a length of material off in a strip.

"Give me your arm," she said, scooting closer and gently taking my hand and pulling it toward her. She wrapped the strip of shirt around my arm as tightly as she could to try and staunch the bleeding, then tore off another small piece of shirt and used it to secure the makeshift bandage.

"Thanks," I said, trying not to sag against her.

"We need to get out of this basement," she said. "Can you walk?"

"I think so. What about you?" I asked, looking at the blood trickling down the side of her face and neck.

"I'm good. At least for now."

She got slowly to her feet, braced herself, and pulled me to mine. We shuffled to the stairs, me leaning on Kat, her arm around my shoulders. I glanced up at the door to the basement. The stairs might as well have been Mount Everest.

"We can do this," she said, putting her hand on the rail.

"Okay," I said, not entirely sure I could. My vision was going grey around the edges.

Kat put her foot on the first step, tightened her grip on my shoulder, and moved us upward. I put one foot in front of the other, trying not to drag on Kat, getting weaker with each step. By the time we reached the top I knew I was almost done. My head sagged to her shoulder. Kat pushed the basement door open, then led us through the house. How she saw enough to guide us in the gloom I had no idea. My eyes fluttered while I struggled to stay conscious and not be more of a burden to my friend.

By the time we got through the front door Kat was swaying too.

"I think this is as far as I go," I said.

My knees hit the porch and I dropped into a pit of darkness.

Chapter 27

B right light filtered through my eyelids as I bounced along, a strap across my chest securing me to something firm that was moving fast.

"What have we got?" I heard a familiar, man's voice next to me say.

"Two females, one with a deep forearm laceration, broken nose, and bruising to the throat, the other with a pretty good head lac, possible mild concussion, and a couple of broken ribs," another man's voice, one I didn't recognize, said.

"Okay, got it. Anything—*Cami*?"

My eyes fluttered open. Wynn was leaning over me, eyebrows tented, face suffused with worry.

Where was I?

I blinked. Wynn had on a white coat. My brain struggled to put two and two together.

I was in the ER. On a gurney.

"Cami, what happened?" He looked to his right, his eyes widening. "Is that Kat?"

He grabbed the side of the gurney and steered me to the left. "*Keoni*! Curtain two!" he bellowed. "Follow me," he said to someone behind him. Must have been talking to the paramedic pushing Kat's gurney.

My gurney came to a stop. The room spun again, the ceiling bright above me.

"We're going to transfer her in three, two, one," I heard Wynn say.

My body slid from the gurney onto an ER bed. Wynn's face hovered above me. "Do you know your blood type?"

I blinked at him.

"A positive," I mumbled.

"Get two liters of A positive, stat," he said to someone I couldn't see.

"Where's Kat?" I whispered.

"She's right here in the next bed," he said. "Keoni!"

"I'm here!" I heard Keoni's voice to my left. "What's—oh my god."

"Take Kat, I've got Cami."

"What the hell happened?" Keoni asked, dashing around my gurney.

"Don't know yet," Wynn said. A nurse in pink scrubs appeared on his right. She handed him a syringe. Another nurse in the same color appeared on my left, an IV needle in her hand. "This is a deep cut, Cami. You've lost a lot of blood. I need to take care of this first. I'm going to numb your arm so I can stitch it up. After that I'll take care of your broken nose. The nurse on your left is going to start an IV so we can get blood and painkillers into you."

"Okay," I mumbled while Wynn poked the needle in a steady row of injections down my arm. I barely registered the pricks. I felt pressure in the top of my left hand when the nurse slid the needle into a vein. She covered it with tape, then pulled an IV pole over. She hung a bag of blood from it, attached a tube to the bottom which she then connected to the IV port in my hand. Next she clamped something onto the tip of my middle finger. I blinked again. My head was fuzzy, making it hard to focus on everything going on around me.

"Hey, Kat, let me look at your head," I heard Keoni say off to my left.

"Push 300 milligrams of clindamycin. I don't want an infection brewing here," Wynn said to the nurse. "Follow that with 10 milligrams of morphine."

"Yes, Doctor Caldwell."

The nurse on Wynn's right swabbed my cut-up arm with Betadine, which left a brownish smear down my arm. Then she handed Wynn a small, curved needle that was threaded with black suture.

"Okay, Cami. Hold still. This is going to take a few minutes."

The ceiling was getting dim. It was like someone was bringing down the lights in a theater right before the movie was about to start. I felt pressure in my left hand when the nurse injected something into the IV port.

"Her pulse is getting thready," the nurse on my left said. She was staring at a monitor I hadn't noticed before. I needed to close my eyes, just for a minute. I was so tired.

"Cami? *Cami*?"

I wanted to answer him, but my mouth wouldn't move. I needed to sleep, just sleep, I thought as the darkness came for me again.

Chapter 28

I woke in a hospital room, sunlight streaming in through the window, its glow muted as it spread across the stark, white walls. The IV was still in my arm, only a bag of clear liquid hung from the pole instead of blood. There was something on my nose. Probably a splint, since it was broken. My right arm was wrapped in bandages. It felt stiff, but it didn't hurt.

My throat hurt a little though. Swallowing made it hurt more. I blinked and looked around the room. There was another bed to my right. Kat was lying in it, head bandaged, escaping hair spread out across the pillow. Her eyes were closed, her breathing deep and even. She had an IV in her arm too.

I wondered what time it was. I could see the sun was still low on the horizon, so early morning. I couldn't remember how we got to the hospital. Had Kat called 911? The gurney, the ER, Wynn flitted through my mind. She must have.

My mind flashed back to the basement, to Bruce and Uriah. Had the police come? Had they found the bodies?

"Cami?" a soft voice said. Wynn's face peered around the door.

I was so glad to see him.

"Hey," I whispered.

"Hey yourself," he said quietly, pushing the door open. He approached the bed and gently slipped his hand into mine. "How are you feeling?"

"Okay, I guess. A little out of it."

"You're lucky that's all you're feeling. You gave us a scare. For a minute there I thought I was going to have to shock you."

"Oh, wow. Sorry about that." I remembered Wynn giving orders, taking care of me. "Thanks for stitching up my arm."

"You're welcome. There should be minimal scarring. I'm pretty good with stitches. Better than Keoni, but don't tell him that," he said, winking at me.

I smiled. "Promise."

"What the heck happened to the two of you?"

"I'd like to know that too," said a voice from the doorway.

Wynn turned toward the voice. A man, who looked to be around thirty, stood just outside the room. His short, wavy brown hair was neatly combed into place over a pale, clean-shaven face. Light blue eyes scanned the room like he was trying to memorize every detail. His eyes tracked from me, to Wynn, to Kat. He wore a dark blue suit, white shirt, and blue and red patterned tie. Brown shoes that needed a bit of polish rounded out his outfit.

"And you are?" Wynn asked.

The man reached into his breast pocket and extracted a brown, leather ID holder. He flipped it open and flashed us a badge.

"Detective Holloway. I was at the crime scene last night. I need to ask Ms. Mitchell and Ms. Howard, the two women that were ambulanced from the scene, a few questions."

My stomach twisted in knots. He said *crime scene*. They had found Bruce and Uriah.

"Can't this wait?" Wynn asked.

"I'd rather do it now," Detective Holloway said, stepping into the room. "While things are still fresh. It won't take long."

"It's okay," I told Wynn.

"Thank you. You're Ms. Mitchell?"

"I am."

Detective Holloway reached into the other side of his jacket and pulled out a small notebook and a ballpoint pen. Kat stirred in the bed, then blinked sleepily at us.

"Morning, Ms. Howard," he said to her.

Kat blinked again at the stranger in the room. "Um, morning?"

"How are you feeling?" Wynn asked, stepping over to Kat's bed.

"Like I got hit by a truck," she said. "Who's he?"

"I'm Detective Holloway, ma'am. I need to ask you ladies some questions about last night."

"Oh," she said, closing her eyes again for a moment. She touched the side of her face, the one with the bruise, and winced. "Last night. I was hoping that was all a bad dream."

"Unfortunately not, ma'am. Can either of you tell me how you came to be at the house at 1251 Colina del Arco Iris?"

"We were abducted. By the two men in the basement," I said.

"Abducted. I see. Can you provide the identities of either of those two men?"

"The older man's name is Bruce Beauregard," Kat said.

"The younger man's name is Uriah," I added. "I don't know his last name."

The detective scribbled in his notebook. "I see. You knew these two men then?"

"I knew Bruce," Kat said. "Neither of us knew Uriah."

"But you know his name."

The detective's eyes were measuring Kat.

"Only because Bruce called him by name," she said, staring back at him. Neither of us mentioned me spying on him in the basement and Ezekiel identifying him. There was no explaining any of that.

"I see. How do you know Mr. Beauregard?"

Kat hesitated for a moment.

"He's in my coven."

The detective's eyebrows went up. So did Wynn's.

"Coven? You mean like *witches*?" Detective Holloway asked.

"Yes, like witches," she said.

"Uh huh. Are you in this coven too?" he asked me.

"No," I said.

"Do either of you have any idea why this Mr. Beauregard, and the other man, Uriah, abducted you?"

"Did you look around the basement?" Kat asked. "Did you *see* what was on the floor?"

"You mean besides two dead bodies? I saw symbols, a book, a bowl, a candle, and blood."

"Those symbols were drawn on the floor for a ritual—"

"A ritual?" He gave Kat a skeptical look. "What kind of ritual?"

"Does it matter? They wanted to contact some kind of spirit. They were nuts. We were meant to be their blood sacrifices."

Detective Holloway frowned, his pen frozen over his notepad.

"I'm sorry, did you say blood sacrifice?"

"That's what I said. They were going to *kill* us."

"And yet, *they're* dead," the detective said.

"Yes, because we fought for our lives." She gestured to her face, then at my injuries. "Clearly."

"One of the men was stabbed in the back. Usually attackers get stabbed in the front of the body."

"That was me," I said. "I stabbed him in the back. He was going to kill Kat." Eventually. As he finished the ritual. "It was the only way I thought I could stop him."

Wynn's eyes got wide. A million questions flitted through them, but he kept quiet.

"I see. And the other man? Mr. Beauregard. How did he come to be stabbed as well?"

"That was me too. We were fighting for the knife. We fell, and the knife got trapped between us."

Holloway's eyes narrowed as he looked at me.

"And conveniently ended up in him."

"It was hardly convenient, but yes."

He scribbled some more.

"So, let me get this straight. Beauregard and Uriah kidnap you, then drag you into a basement where they plan on performing a ritual. To contact some kind of spirit." He eyed us both again. "You struggle with them, kill them both, and then escape the house and call for help. Is that about right?"

"That's pretty much it, yes," Kat said.

"Is there anything else I should know?"

"Yes. They killed my friend Greg Wattanabe."

Holloway's eyebrows lifted.

"Greg Wattanabe." The detective scribbled again. "And how do you know they killed him?"

"Bruce admitted it while we were in the basement," I said.

"I see. Was Greg Wattanabe also a member of your coven?" he asked Kat.

"Yes," she replied.

I remembered what else Bruce said in the basement.

"Not just Greg," I told Kat. "They killed your friends Evelyn, Merriam, and Leonard too."

"*What?*" Kats eyes were wide and round, pleading with me to tell her it wasn't true.

"Bruce told me that too. He said they killed them the night they took us."

"Oh my god." Kat's face crumpled when she began to sob. Wynn sat on the edge of the bed, and took her hand. She gripped it tightly as her body shook.

"There are three more victims?" Detective Holloway asked, eyebrows still raised, his eyes shifting between me and Kat.

"That I know of," I said.

"There were no other bodies down in that basement."

"Greg was killed in his house. Then they burned it down. Merriam and Leonard were killed at her home, I think. I'm not sure about Evelyn."

"Were these also members of your coven?" he asked Kat.

She nodded, still too overcome to speak.

"Did Mr. Beauregard give you any indication as to why he allegedly killed these three individuals? Or why he seems to have targeted members of his coven?"

"He said something about it being a part of the ritual," I said.

I left the rest out. It wasn't like I could tell him about the spirits in the basement, or Ezekiel. If I did, he would look at me like I was nuts, and I'd probably end up in the psych ward.

"Okay, then," he said, his pen scribbling furiously again. "I need addresses to corroborate this story with Santa Theresa PD. And recover any bodies."

Was this guy with the state police? Santa Theresa's police department was really small. Maybe they didn't have detectives.

"Evelyn lived at 1480 Dysart Street," Kat said, her chest hitching. "Merriam lived at 560 Westchester. Greg's death has already been reported."

"I'll check with the local P.D. about that too. Is there anything else I should know about?"

"Not that I can think of," I said. There was nothing else to add that he would believe.

"The book you found," said Kat. "That's mine. They stole it. I need it back."

Detective Holloway's eyes fixed on Kat.

"They stole your book? Why?"

"They needed it to complete the ritual," she said.

"They needed a book *you* own to complete this ritual. Which requires a *blood* sacrifice. May I ask why you would have such a book, Ms. Howard?"

"I collect occult books. I sell most of them in my bookstore."

"And this one? Was it for sale? Couldn't they have just bought it?"

"No. This was in my private collection. It's not a book I would ever resell. For obvious reasons."

"I see." He stopped writing and pinched the bridge of his nose. I thought I heard him mutter something about always getting the crazy cases. "The book, along with everything else, is in evidence right now. Once our investigation is complete, and you've been cleared of any wrongdoing, you can file a claim to get it back." He flipped through his notebook, reviewing what he had written down. "Alright. That's everything for now. Don't leave town. I'm pretty sure I'm going to have more questions for you later."

He took a business card out of the ID wallet and handed it to me. It said *Detective Dashiell Holloway* in neat black typeface. Underneath his name was *San Luis Obispo County Sheriff's Department. Homicide Division*. Underneath that was a phone number.

"If you remember anything else pertinent, call me. You too, Ms. Howard."

"Sure," I said.

He nodded at Wynn. "Doctor Caldwell."

A wave of relief washed over me after he left. For a while I thought he was going to charge us with something. I hoped he concluded we had clearly acted in self-defense.

"Holy cow, Cami. You guys went through all that?" Wynn asked, worried eyes fixed on me again.

"It was a rough night," I said.

"That's an understatement," Kat said, snuffling. Wynn patted her on the hand, then placed it back on the bed. He got up and came over to me.

"I'm so sorry you two went through that. You're both going to be okay though. I want to keep you here overnight, just for observation, but you can go home tomorrow."

"Can't we go home today? I need to check on my cat. I need to know he's alive," Kat said, her eyes frantic again.

I had totally forgotten about Wizard. I remembered the big ball of fur lying on my floor, motionless. I wanted to leave too so that I could check on Deedee and see Bandit. I missed him so much right now it hurt.

"I can do that," Wynn said. "My shift is over in a half an hour."

"Wizard is at my house," I said. "The front door should be open." I doubted Bruce and Uriah had locked up after they kidnapped us.

"Alright." He leaned over and kissed my forehead. "I'll call you when I get there, okay? Oh, here." He reached into the pocket of his doctor's coat. "This was in your back pocket," he said, handing me my phone. "I'll have a nurse bring up your clothes. They're still in a bag in the ER."

"Thanks."

I fervently hoped Wizard was alright. I didn't want another name to be added to the list of already too many casualties.

Chapter 29

Wynn was as good as his word. My phone rang an hour later. Wizard was okay. Limping and agitated as all get out, but alive. Wynn said the cat yowled at him for almost five minutes. He examined Wizard, but couldn't find anything broken. He was able to feed the feline, and Wizard even allowed Wynn to pet him a little. I didn't tell him that Wizard was more than an ordinary cat, that he was Kat's familiar. That was a discussion that could happen another time. Or not.

Kat and I spent the rest of the day in the hospital. We didn't talk much about what happened in the basement. It was too raw. We both just wanted to forget, at least for a little while.

Wynn drove us home the next day. Kat scooped a waiting Wizard up as soon as she got in the door. She buried her face in his fur, her shoulders shaking gently. He purred like a motor boat again.

"Thank you for making sure he was okay," Kat said to Wynn. Her eyes were red rimmed and full of tears as she held Wizard close.

"My pleasure. Looks like he's as happy to see you. I think bed rest and lots of cuddles are in order for both of you. Doctor's orders."

Kat gave him a grateful smile.

"I have no problem with that," she said. "Thanks again for everything. Tell Keoni thanks too."

"I will."

We could hear Wizard's continued purrs as he and Kat left the room.

Wynn turned and wrapped his arms around me. I leaned into him, relishing the safety and comfort his embrace provided.

"Bed rest for you too," he said, stepping back and letting go. He pulled a pill bottle out of his coat pocket and handed it to me. "I got painkillers for you both at the hospital pharmacy. Take one every four to six hours as needed."

"Thanks." I hoped I wasn't going to need them. I really didn't like taking pharmaceuticals. However, if my arm and nose kept throbbing the way they were, I was going to reconsider.

"Off to bed now, alright?"

"Okay," I said. I was still weak, and a little lightheaded.

"C'mon," he said, taking my hand. "Let's get you tucked in. You look like you might faint on the way. Which way is your bedroom?"

A blush crept over my cheeks. We were nowhere near that stage in our relationship, and I wasn't used to having guys in my bedroom.

"This way," I said, leading him down the hall.

My bedroom was an ode to the beach. White walls were the backdrop for an aqua bedspread decorated with a white seashell print and matching aqua throw pillows. An overstuffed chair covered with similar, aqua fabric sat in the corner next to a standing lamp and a small table. An armoire that was painted white rested against the wall perpendicular to the bed, and a large oil painting of waves crashing over a beach hung over the bed.

Wynn peeled pack the bedspread and duvet and held them so I could climb in. He tucked the duvet around me, then sat down on the bed.

"Are you going to be okay?" he asked. "That was some experience you two had."

I nodded, although I wasn't really sure. My stomach hitched every time I thought of Bruce and Uriah. And that I killed them.

"Listen, if you need to talk, I'm always here for you. I can't even begin to imagine what you went through. Being kidnapped, having to fight for your life." He brushed a strand of hair from my face. "I'm so sorry you had to go through that."

"Me too. I'm even sorrier for Kat. She lost four good friends."

"That's rough," Wynn said, his eyes sad. "Did you know any of them?"

"I met Greg the night before he died. I didn't know any of the others."

"I wonder why those guys picked you two for the ritual instead of the others."

I couldn't tell him that they wanted to sacrifice me because I was a medium. I knew exactly what kind of reaction that would get. One day I wanted to tell Wynn about my ability, but not yet. We needed a stronger foundation and more time together before I even contemplated that. I wasn't sure what the benchmark for that was, but maybe after we'd been together for a few months, at least. By then hopefully he would know me well enough that he wouldn't think I was either crazy, or just making up some wild story.

"I don't know. People who want to perform blood rituals do so for their own reasons."

"For sure." His eyes turned from sad to worried. "You want me to stay for a while? I don't need to be back at the hospital until tonight."

"That's okay. You should go home. I'll probably take one of the painkillers and spend most of the day sleeping anyway."

That was partly true. While I wanted to rest, I really wanted to get down to the bookstore.

"Okay. I'll call you later and check on you."

He leaned over and gave me a gentle kiss.

"Thank you for taking care of us, and bringing us home," I said.

"Anytime."

After he left, I pushed back the duvet and forced myself to sit up. I did plan on resting, but not until I got down to Beltane Books and checked on Bandit and Deedee. That was my number one priority.

When I walked into the store, Eve was toward the back helping a customer. Kat had called her from the hospital and asked her to man the fort for a few days. I didn't see Deedee or Bandit anywhere.

I hurried through the doorway that led to the bathroom, kitchen, and storeroom so Eve wouldn't see me. I didn't want to have to explain why my face looked the way it did. The kitchen and bathroom were empty. The only place they could be was the storeroom.

I found Deedee sitting on a box, her side to the door, her hand on Bandit's shoulder. Bandit's head swiveled around when he heard my footsteps.

"Rooooooooo!"

Bandit ran to me, tail wagging. My eyes welled up. I wanted to hug my dog so much it hurt.

"Cami." Deedee stood and came over. "Is everything okay now? Bandit left for a little while, but then he came back. I kind of thought that since he came back you were successful, but I wanted to stay just in case."

"Yes, Deedee," I said quietly so Eve wouldn't hear me. "You and others are safe."

"Thank you, Cami. And thank you, Bandit, for being with me."

She reached down and scratched him behind the ears. I wished just as much that I could hug my friend. I had to settle for a wave as Deedee vanished.

"Ready to go home, buddy?"

"Rowwwrrr," he said, ears pricked and tail still wagging.

"Yeah, me too."

I drove us home, anticipating a long rest. I couldn't cuddle with my dog, but having him near me was enough.

Kat stayed with me for another week. She had mixed feelings about going home. She was still trying to decide whether she wanted to continue to live in her house, or find a new place.

We went to Greg's funeral together, where Kat said her final good-bye. After everyone left, I gave her Greg's message. That made her cry more than the service. There had been so much loss for her in so little time.

I was sorry for Greg's death, and the death of the others, but thankful that Kat and I were still alive. If things had gone differently we would be somewhere I didn't even want to contemplate, and Bruce, Uriah, and Ezekiel would be bringing hell to Santa Theresa. But they were gone, and my friends, my dog, and the town I loved were safe.

And, I had a new love in my life, someone who made me feel special, and normal. Sometimes you had to be grateful for what you had.

I was. In spades.

The End.

Next in the Series

Cami's adventures continue in Spirit Whispers, out now, and available on Amazon.

https://a.co/d/4vyPqmt

Turn the page to read the first chapter...

Spirit Whispers, Chapter 1

C ampus seemed more crowded than usual today, maybe because half of the University of California SantaTheresa's student body was pushing their way out of Declan Hall at the same time. I'd been hovering twenty feet from the entrance for almost five minutes and was still no closer to getting inside. If I didn't get in soon, I was going to be late for my meeting with my advisor. He had told me he had news about my master's thesis, and had hinted that it was not only exciting, but maybe even a gamechanger.

Finally, the flow ebbed and I wove between the other students to get to the ornate, turn of the last century Victorian door. I was almost through it when I bumped into a redheaded undergrad with purple socks peeking out from under his floods, that clashed with his orange UCST t-shirt.

"Hey, what's your hurry, Blondie?" he asked, his eyes drifting over my blue peasant top and jeans.

I ignored him and ran up the stairs to the third floor, gripping the carved wooden handrail so that I didn't get knocked bum over teakettle by one of the students that was flying down the stairs like their hair was on fire, and coming so close to me that they were about to turn me into a human pinball. Dr. Lindquist's office was the fourth door down the hall on the right. The sign on his door read, 'Dr. Byron Lindquist, Psychology Department Chair.'

"Come in," he said after I knocked. "Cami. Right on time."

"Good afternoon, Dr. Lindquist."

"How are you today?" He gestured for me to sit down in the old, creased leather chair that faced his desk. His pale blue eyes peered at me over his reading glasses. "How are classes going?"

I slid my worn, red backpack off my shoulder and sat.

"Fine so far. I'm particularly enjoying Theories of Personality and Psychology of Deviance."

He chuckled.

"Since your master's thesis is about serial killers, and what makes them tick, I'm not surprised those two would appeal to you."

"They're endlessly fascinating. We're going to be looking at some interesting case studies soon that could correlate to my thesis. They'll definitely help my research."

"Speaking of," he said, leaning forward in his seat with an excited gleam in his eye, "remember when we talked last year about the possibility of you interviewing a serial killer?"

"Yes, sir. There are some incarcerated up in San Quentin, and Pelican Bay. I thought I might be able to arrange something over the holiday break. I was planning to start the request process soon."

"Well, you're in luck. There's one a lot closer to home now. I started greasing the wheels a few months ago for you to interview one."

My jaw dropped as I gaped at Dr. Lindquist.

"You did? Really?"

He grinned at my slack-jawed surprise, the laugh lines around his eyes deepening.

"Yes. I didn't want to say anything in case I wasn't successful, but I was. I've been trying to set up an interview for you with Henry Spaulding. As you probably know, he was transferred to Cabrillo State Penitentiary."

"Oh, *wow*. Thank you, sir."

"I've been speaking with the warden at Cabrillo State. I explained your thesis, and that you're trying to dig deeper into why people become killers, and he found it very interesting. He was open to the idea of you speaking to Spaulding, which is more luck for you because interviews with serial killers are rarely granted by the system. He finally agreed to share your interest in an interview with Spaulding."

"Yes, sir. I think that's going to be the biggest obstacle. Spaulding doesn't grant interviews."

"Well, in your case, he has. The warden told me yesterday. You still have to fill out the forms and questionnaires required by the prison system, but the warden assured me they would be approved expeditiously. I'll email you the link his secretary provided."

A mixture of excited and apprehensive butterflies fluttered around in my stomach. For some unknown reason, Henry Spaulding had agreed to let me interview him. *Me*, a lowly grad student. I was going to be face to face with one of California's most elusive serial killers. If my interview went well, I might be able to learn something from him that I couldn't read online or in a textbook. He had revealed very little to law enforcement so far, and there was only limited information available about him. I knew he wasn't going to pour all his secrets out to me, but still. Maybe I would get lucky and get some small nugget. Plus, just being able to talk to a living serial killer would help my thesis.

"Thank you so much, Dr. Lindquist. I wasn't expecting to be able to do this so soon. I *really* appreciate it."

"You're welcome," he said as he leaned back in his chair again. "It's rare for a student in their first year of the master's program to get an opportunity like this. A lot of times prisons only allow access to the police and the mental health professionals they have on staff."

"I'll take it," I said, flushed with excited anticipation. "This is an amazing opportunity. Although..."

"Although?"

"I'm wondering why Spaulding agreed to the interview. From what I've read, he has given almost none. He's been questioned extensively by law enforcement, and psychiatrists, but has rarely agreed to voluntary interviews. Why me?"

Dr. Lindquist shrugged, and blinked at me through his spectacles.

"Who knows? Maybe the idea of being interviewed by someone outside the system that isn't some nosy reporter looking to make a name for themselves was appealing."

"Could be," I said. I chewed on my lower lip while I processed the prospect of the interview. "That doesn't mean he's going to tell me anything significant. He might just want to play head games."

"Definitely a possibility. Or, he was piqued when he found out you're a female grad student. He doesn't get to see many women in prison, particularly young ones."

"True. I'm over ten years older than his usual victims, but maybe I'm better than nothing. Perhaps that will give me an edge when I'm interviewing him."

"It's hard to know what's going on in his mind. The best you can do is prepare, and be professional while you're there. Watch his body language. Listen for what he's not saying. Sometimes the most innocuous statement can mean a lot more coming from a mind as disturbed as his."

"He wouldn't be the first serial killer to be elusive," I said. "Ted Bundy was a master at it."

"He was, although he was a lot smarter than Spaulding. Henry Spaulding is cunning, but has shown evidence of cognitive challenges since childhood."

"You don't have to be a genius to kill people."

"No, you don't," Dr. Lindquist agreed. "Although a lot of these types of killers have above average IQ's. In Spalding's case, what he lacks in intelligence, he makes up for in brutality."

A shudder shimmied from my shoulders down my back.

"We're all lucky he's behind bars. Little girls everywhere are safer for it."

Henry Spalding's victims of choice were girls between the ages of ten and fourteen. He was suspected to have been active for around ten years. Plenty of time to commit a lot of murders.

"Definitely," he said. "How many girls have they tied to him?"

"So far only three, but they suspect he may have killed dozens more. He's a calling card killer. *The White Lily Killer*. He leaves a white lily at the murder scene. They haven't found most of the bodies so far though, except those of his first two victims, and his last victim. With the last one he was sloppier, and killed her in a hurry."

"Which means either his MO evolved, or he's unraveling." Dr. Lindquist said.

"So it would seem. It's hard to know without being able to examine the other victims, and where he killed them. The police never found his killing ground. That's where they think he killed most of his victims, since they never found any other bodies."

"He's a strange one," Dr. Lindquist said. "Some killers have killing grounds where they commit their murders, then dump the body somewhere else. Spaulding has hidden his bodies well."

"He has. The first one was murdered almost a hundred miles north of here, and it seemed like he was still honing his skills as a killer. The second was much more methodical, and forensics determined that he was organized, and took his time. The last one, found just outside of White Rock, was killed in a hurry. It was as if he couldn't, or didn't want to take his time. He still left his calling card though."

"Maybe he felt like he couldn't make it back to wherever he killed the other girls," Dr. Lindquist said.

"Could be. The police believe strongly that he has a killing ground somewhere, and that's why they haven't found the other bodies. Although I would imagine he would have to take the bodies somewhere, right? Unless he keeps them around for some reason. He wouldn't be the first serial killer to do that. John Wayne Gacy had a basement full of bodies."

"Well, hopefully you can get a glimpse into what makes this man tick when you interview him. Even if you don't learn much more from him that isn't textbook, it will still be a fascinating experience."

"*Definitely*. Thanks again, Dr. Lindquist."

"You're very welcome. I look forward to hearing all about it."

I left his office and retreated across campus to my car .I still couldn't believe it. I was going to interview Henry Spaulding. I was going to sit face to face with someone who's mind held endless fascination for me. The question was, what was stirring in that mind?

Author Social Information

Follow the author at:

Facebook: T. N. Trainer Author
Instagram: authortntrainer
Bluesky: authortntrainer.bsky.social
Threads: authortntrainer
Website: www.authortntrainer.com